THE

PLANTING

OF THE

PENNY HEDGE

ISBN: 9781070350479

First published 2019 by Follow This Publishing, Yorkshire (UK)
Text © 2019 Chris Turnbull
Cover Design © 2019 Joseph Hunt of Incredibook Design

For Jean & Trevor

To Edna

Happy Reading!

Turnbull
x
2o9.

ALSO BY CHRIS TURNBULL

The Vintage Coat
Carousel

D: Darkest Beginnings
D: Whitby's Darkest Secret
D: Revenge Hits London

It's Beginning To Look A Lot Like Christmas
A Home For Emy
Emy Gets A Sister

A Detective Matthews Novel

-1-

The Planting

of the

Penny Hedge

Chris Turnbull

"Every blade has two edges; he who wounds with one wounds himself with the other."
— **Victor Hugo**

Prologue

'If this is another one of your practical jokes young Peter I will not be at all impressed.' PC Williams scold the young boy. It was six o'clock in the morning and Peter, a ten-year-old harbour assistant, had woken up the constable by banging on his front door repeatedly until the old officer answered.

'I ain't messin' I promise. Hurry up.'

'Okay, okay…lead the way.' Williams groaned as he threw on his boots and coat. Williams had been pranked by the young lad before, and was it not for the paled shocked expression on his face he may not have taken him seriously.

'I was walkin' along the cliff top sir, headed to the harbour for work and heard shouting from the beach below.'

'What was it?' Williams replied, already breathless trying to keep up with the young lad.

'Old man shouting for 'elp. I went down to see and he told me to fetch a copper. I knew you lived close so thought it be quicker than heading to the station.'

'Where exactly is it you are taking me?' PC Williams asked as Peter led him onto what looked like a deserted Whitby beach, a long stretch of brownish sand that was sat alongside the jagged clifftops. The beach was covered in seaweed, shells and the occasional jellyfish. As they sped across the beach towards the waters edge, which was receding in the early daylight, PC Williams finally saw the elderly gentleman who was stood waiting for them. He was wrapped up warm against the early morning sea breeze, a King Charles spaniel attached to the lead in his hand. He gave a wave to the constable as though trying to grab his attention, but Williams had already seen him and was running in his direction.

Approaching the man Williams did not address

him immediately, but instead his gaze was drawn down to the ground beside him. His eyes bulged with what was laid out before them both. He had to look away, covering his mouth he gagged as though to vomit, but nothing came out. He went to look again but immediately began to gag again.

'Peter, I need you to run back to the police station for me please.'

'But Sir...'

'Now Peter! There will be somebody there, tell them where I am and that I need the chief here immediately. Go! Run!' Peter took off back along the sand as quickly as he could, turning back only once, before disappearing in the direction of town.

'What is your name sir?' the constable asked the elderly man.

'O'Sullivan, Ernest O'Sullivan. I live just down from the Pavilion on Havelock Place.' Williams looked over his shoulder, the pavilion that dominated the cliff side was built from red brick and had only opened the previous year. Williams thought it was an eyesore against the beautiful coastline and spoilt the natural cliff faces. He brought his gaze back to Mr O'Sullivan, he didn't want to look back to the ground next to him, but he knew he had to. There laid on the sand was the body of a man. Dressed in a simple navy blue long sleeved shirt and black trousers, the lifeless man donned heavy boots on his feet and was completely soaked. The tide, which was now retracting, still lapped as his feet. The dead man was not simply laid on the sand as though washed in by the tide, but in actual fact secured down to it. He lay on his back with his arms raised up to his face. A small fence like structure, no taller than a foot, and made of small wooden sticks, held the man in place by his neck and wrists.

'Do you know this man?' Williams asked the Mr O'Sullivan, again trying to avoid looking at the dead man.

'No sir, I walked passed a while back when the tide was further in and didn't see anything. But heading home the sea had gone out a wee bit and I could see the top half of him. It's gone out more now.'

'What time did you leave your house?'

'Will be over half an hour ago, something like that.' Mr O'Sullivan's voice was croaky and he began to shiver in the cool breeze. His dog too was beginning to shake.

'Could you write your full address down on my pad for me, just in case we need to contact you for further questions?' Mr O'Sullivan took the pad and pencil. As he wrote a figure appeared on the cliffside, it was the chief of police. He could be seen hurrying across the beach at full speed alone.

'What the blazers is this Williams?' The chief's deep booming voice echoed off the cliffs. 'Do we have an ID?'

'No sir, this is Mr O'Sullivan, found the body not too long ago. Doesn't know who he is.' The chief leaned into the body for a closer look. Williams admired his strong stomach, he had still only managed brief glimpses himself.

'I'm curious to know if he died from drowning or if he was already dead before being put here,' the chief stated, still lingering over the body. 'Certainly not anybody I know. I'm surprised this wooden structure around him didn't get taken away with the tide, it doesn't look strong enough to withstand a single tide; and a big strapping young man like this surely wouldn't of found it a struggle being restrained in these twigs.'

'What the hell happened?' Williams said under his breath, the chief did not hear him. He took a more longing look at the corpse. His clothes were drenched and clinging to the body. Despite his clear youth the sea water had dried out his skin, causing it to be wrinkled with red blotches all over it, as well as white dried out dead skin from the salt. It had certainly made him look much older than he undoubtedly was.

'Is back up coming to help us move him?' Williams asked.

'Too bloody right, I ain't moving this fella with just you. This obviously isn't a normal crime scene now is it Williams, the tide will have washed all the bloody evidence away; so we'll have to get him off to the coroner to be checked over as quickly as we can.' He lit a cigarette and offered one to both Williams and Mr O'Sullivan, both of whom refused.

'Poor bastard,' he continued, puffing on his cigarette, 'Back up better bloody hurry up, I don't want the Gazette catching wind of this before we can move him.'

CHAPTER I

THURSDAY 7TH MAY 1891 - YORK

Benjamin Matthews slammed his suitcase closed in anger and lit a cigarette to calm himself. He sat on the edge of his single bed and inhaled his smoke until his temper mellowed. He was dressed in smart trousers, clean shirt and waistcoat; his usual attire. His short brown hair was slicked back and he was clean shaven. He was tall and lean and had the most striking green eyes that stood out from across the room, and a smile that could charm most. He took out a pocket watch from his waistcoat pocket, originally his grandfather's, which he had inherited after his passing, and checked the time, almost time to leave.

Outside the window of his rented room the bells of York Minster began to chime midday. Matthews stood and glanced out of his window for the last time. He had enjoyed living in York for the past two years; the view itself was outstanding of the towering Minster. Having one of the largest cathedrals in northern Europe as his daily view he thought of as a treat, with its towers dominating every other building in the city, and its gothic architecture making it by far the most stunning building Matthews had ever laid eyes on. Today the blue skies framed the Minster magnificently. In the street below horse and carts raced along among the hustle and bustle of the cities many residents, all going about their everyday business. He had his single suitcase ready to go.

Matthews was a police officer, he had trained since being a teenager; and had moved to York just over two years ago when he was offered a constabulary position. Now twenty-four he finally felt as though he had made it on his own. He had achieved his dream of being an officer just as his father had and was living somewhere he loved. Everything was going just had he had hoped; that was up until the previous week when he had been called into the chiefs office to be given some news. His father, head of police at Whitby, had put in a request to have him transferred back to Whitby as soon as possible. Presuming that this was what Matthews wanted the chief simply signed the paperwork necessary to allow it, and called a meeting with him a couple of days later to let Matthews know when he was leaving. The chief was taken by surprise when he was faced with confusion and anger about this. Matthews had never spoken to his father about returning to Whitby, and it certainly wasn't something he would gladly agree to. After the meeting he was irate with his father for not discussing it with him first, he didn't want to be back in Whitby under his father's control, or even worse, seen as the chief's son. In York he had the freedom to be himself, and his achievements felt like his own.

His final week in York had passed much quicker than he could have imagined. He didn't have much belongings to take with him, with the majority of his clothes fitting into one medium sized leather suitcase. He had been renting a single room above a bakery on High Petergate, he would certainly miss the smell of the freshly baked bread each morning.

Eventually a carriage pulled up outside, a small cart with an open seated area and pulled by a single brown horse. The sight of this cart made Matthews pleased the rain that had been constant all morning had finally stopped. He grabbed his suitcase and put on his navy coloured knee length coat and black bowler hat and made his way down the rickety stairs.

He stopped briefly in the bakery to hand over his keys to Mrs Lindgren, his landlady and bakery owner, before heading out onto the noisy street. Being Thursday lunchtime, the city was at its busiest and the morning rain had left behind a petrichor scent in the air, which Matthews couldn't resist filling his nostrils with one last time. He hopped over a puddle in the doorway and waved down the driver in acknowledgement who was waiting for him.

'Afternoon Matthews,' the middle-aged carriage driver greeted him. 'I suppose this'll be our last ride together?' The man, whose name was Neville, was a regular face around York and knew more people by name than Matthews thought possible. He always seemed to remember everything about people, and would often ask after his family by name, despite never meeting them, or asking after Matthews latest investigation.

'Afternoon Neville, yes I'm afraid this is me leaving. Could we drop into the police station before you take me for the train, I need to drop off my badge and uniform?'

'Sure thing sir.'

Neville strapped down the suitcase to the back of the carriage. Matthews, who was also carrying a suit bag, laid this on the carriage seat next to him; it contained his police uniform which he had worn for the last time just the previous day. As they drove through the streets of York Matthews barely took any of it in to begin with. His hand rested on the suit bag and he could feel his badge inside. Determined not to put on a sour face, Matthews plastered a fake smile and brought his attention back to the passing buildings and streets so he could admire them for the last time in who knows how long.

It was only a short distance to the train station,

with the police station on route for him to hand over his things, he had been more than willing to walk but the York police chief had insisted he be given a lift. Neville spoke only to the horse as they made their way along the road. Matthews turned back occasionally to look at the Minster, which he felt sad to be leaving, and as they crossed Lendal bridge the Minster was lost from sight and Matthews sighed with anguish.

At the police station Matthews ran inside with the suit bag, shouting back to Neville to wait for him.

'Morning Jean,' he greeted the receptionist who always wore bright dresses and fussed over all of the officers like she was their mother, 'is the chief in?'

'I'm sorry lad he's in meetings all morning.' She took the suit bag from him and placed it on a hook in the wall behind her. 'That it then, you off today?'

'Headed to the station right now, Jean.'

'Oh come here.' And she came from around the counter and pulled him in for a hug. She barely came up to his shoulder, even in her small heels. 'The chief is disappointed to be losing you.'

'I best go; Neville is waiting outside for me.' And

with that Matthews made a swift exit from the station, in the hope to escape before anybody else saw him, the last thing he wanted was any more pity goodbyes to be given.

Back outside and Neville drove the horse drawn carriage around to the train station entrance, where he pulled up right outside the door. Matthews bid him a farewell and went to pay him for the ride but Neville refused the money.

'Chiefs already covered this one, mate,' he said with a smirk. 'Now clear off before you miss the bloody thing.' He sniggered at his own sarcasm. Matthews shook the man by the hand before reluctantly making his way inside. His train was due to leave in fifteen minutes and so he found himself somewhere to sit whilst he waited.

Sitting on a hard, uncomfortable bench beside the track, the fifteen minutes seemed to last a lifetime. People of all walks of life were rushing around the busy station as trains arrived and departed from all across the station. The smell of burning coal and oily engines filled Matthews nostrils, he quite liked it; train travel was certainly his favourite mode of transport. He had even considered being a train driver in his youth, but it was the police that really excited him when it came to a career.

The tracks in front of him began to vibrate and shudder, and moments later the sound of the steam engine clanging along the tracks echoed throughout the station. The platform was engulfed in smoke upon its arrival and Matthews stood and waited for the smoke to clear before he made for the carriage. A handful of people disembarked and even fewer people got on board. The small steam engine pulled along three passenger carriages, yet the train was so quiet that they could have all fit into one quite easily. Upon entering the first carriage Matthews stopped and hoisted his suitcase up above his head in order to place it onto one of the luggage racks at the end of the carriage. He had failed to see the young lady boarding behind him and accidently elbowed her straight in the chest. She gasped in horror, stumbling back somewhat as she clasped her chest in shock, she had been slightly winded and when opening her mouth to speak no words came out. Matthews dropped his suitcase to the floor and spun to see the ladies shaken face as she held her panting chest.

'My sincere apologies madam, I did not see you behind me.' His face was equally shocked as hers.

'N… No harm done.' She tried to smile through the pain and still gasping to breathe. 'My own fault for rushing on so quickly.'

The woman was approximately a foot shorter than Matthews; she had a deep purple floor length dress on and wore white lace gloves. Her blonde hair, which was tied up, peeked out beneath her large brimmed hat. She had blue eyes and was clearly younger than Matthews by a couple of years. She had a citrus scent to her and her small leather travel suitcase, which she had dropped in the commotion, looked equally expensive as her dress and hat.

'I assure you the blame lies completely on me,' Matthews replied. He swung his suitcase up onto the rack so as to clear a path for the woman. He then retrieved her bag from the floor and handed it back to her before standing aside and making a polite hand gesture encouraging her to go on ahead. 'By the way,' he said as she passed him, 'I am PC Benjamin Matthews. I would like you to know I do not make it a habit to assault ladies on a regular occurrence.' He held out his hand to her to shake and smiled, hoping she would know he was simply trying to humour his error. She smiled back and returned the hand shake.

'I should hope not constable; it would not do you or your department much favour.' Her smirk told him that she too was making humour out of the situation.

'Are you headed to Whitby, Miss….erm?'

'My name is Grace, Grace Clayson, and yes I live in Whitby with my fiancé. Good afternoon constable.' She gave him another friendly smile and took a seat towards the middle of the carriage. As Matthews took a seat closer to the door the train began to pull away from the platform.

'Well then…' he spoke to himself in a whisper, watching the platform from the window '…back home to Whitby it is then.'

The train left the city of York behind and was soon surrounded by luscious green countryside. A paperboy walked along the moving train selling copies of *The Press* which Matthews purchased a copy of, and he read through the many articles between looking out of the window. The seats of the half empty train were certainly not the comfiest, however the views across the Yorkshire moors certainly made up for it. He found himself occasionally glancing in Grace's direction, but she never looked back at him. She was reading a book and didn't move the entire journey.

Matthews remembered his last visit to Whitby, only a month ago. It was to attend the funeral of his mother. He had tried to forget that day the best he could, he hadn't cried at all since finding out she had died, and even his sister's sobs throughout the ceremony didn't seem to cause him to join her. He loved his mother dearly, and felt guilty for not shedding any tears for her passing. He had only stayed the one night for her funeral, he couldn't bear to be around his family's contagious sorrow and decided to return to York and back to work where his mind would be occupied.

As the steam locomotive pulled into Whitby station over two hours later, the sense of relief from passengers was apparent.

CHAPTER 2

The train stopped at the platform in a cloud of its own smoke and the screeching of its old rusty brakes. Matthews wavered for a moment before leaving his seat, he wished he could remain on the train in order to return to York. Grace, who had been sitting only a couple of seats ahead of him the whole way, gave him a friendly smile as she passed him on her way to the exit. He quickly jumped from his seat and retrieved his bag from the luggage rack and followed her out onto the platform.

'Would you like me to call you a carriage?' Matthews asked with a hint of hesitation.

'Oh,' she seemed almost taken aback by his question, 'no it is quite alright, my fiancé should be outside waiting for me. It was very nice to meet you constable.' She turned and briskly walked along the short platform and out onto the street. Matthews left her to rush on ahead prior to heading out himself. He wasn't expecting anybody to be waiting for him anyway.

The sun was shining through the cloud filled sky, and the salty sea breeze caught the back of Matthews throat the moment he stepped out onto the street. The cries of seagulls rung like sirens from up above. The busy streets, although not quite as busy as York, were bustling with people going about their business. Horse manure littered the roads, whilst road cleaners, consisting of a man shovelling up the mess and collecting it on the back of his cart, struggled to keep up with the constant deposits. Between the manure, salty sea air, the nearby harbour and the hundreds of chimneys puffing out black sooty smoke, Whitby was a constant array of odours. Yet despite this, Matthews couldn't help but feel like he was home. He had been born in Whitby and grew up in the town. His family had been from this area for numerous generations and he felt as though he knew the town better than he knew himself.

As expected, there was nobody waiting to greet him outside of the train station, he saw Grace being helped into a nearby carriage by a thuggish looking man with a large black beard and bowler hat; her fiancé no doubt. He couldn't help but wonder why she had been travelling alone from York, but knew this was none of his business and decided to put her from his mind.

With no key to his father's house, where he presumed he would be staying until he could make other arrangements, he decided to make his way straight to the police station in hope to get the key and return to the house to unwind. It may not have been the longest of journeys but he felt exhausted, and some time to himself whist his father and sister were out was just what he needed. As he walked, he mumbled to himself his annoyance at the whole thing, his father had not even sent him a letter before or after putting in his transfer request. He had not enquired when he would be arriving or anything.

It was a short walk to the police station; a grand building made of large red stone slabs with huge imposing windows along the front. Matthews walked straight through the front door and gave a quick 'hello' to the receptionist before letting himself through to the back; he had been here many times and was known by almost everyone. When he arrived outside is father's office, his secretary looked up from her typewriter as Matthews marched through the outer office and walked straight passed her and into his father's office unannounced. She did nothing to stop him, and he was sure she had smirked at his charged efforts to make an unannounced entrance.

'How dare you put in a transfer for me without even discussing it with me first.' He slammed the door behind himself, aware that the secretary just outside had stopped typing. Dropping his suitcase next to the door, he marched over to the enormous oak desk his father sat behind and slammed both hands down onto the desk causing a loud bang.

'Ah, you are finally here,' his father responded as

though his son had casually walked in the room. He was an equally tall man with a well-kept beard, dark hair that was greying on the sides and wore a smart suit, with a pocket watch chain hanging from his jacket pocket. It was clear to look at the two men to see they were related. 'Sit down boy I have plenty to tell you. I thought you might have arrived last night, but no matter you are here now.' His voice was deep and gravely.

'Pops, you are not listening to me.' Matthews tried to keep a civilized tone with his father but he knew he would keep ignoring his annoyance if he didn't persist. He took the seat opposite without invitation. The office was a large oval shaped room with bookshelves and windows circling the desk.

'Yes, I am listening to you, and you know why I did it. I told you when I last saw you I was going to put in the transfer and…'

'And I told you I didn't want it.' Matthews cut off his father, his voice still raised. 'Don't use mothers funeral last month as an excuse. I told you at the church, I told you at the wake, and I told you at the train station before I returned to York that I did not want to be transferred here. You know how I feel about the force seeing me as the chief's son, and yet despite what I want you went ahead and did it anyway. As usual it is about what you want and screw everybody else.'

'Your mother's funeral was a difficult time for all the family.' His father spoke in a hushed tone. 'It is not just myself wanting you closer, your sister Charlotte and brother Robert have been asking me about you returning ever since the funeral.' The chief gave out a long sigh. 'However, you are here now and I have great news.'

'I fail to see any positives, but what I want to know is where I will be living, you have not communicated with me at all during this transfer, so I presume I will be moving back home until I can find something?'

'Actually,' the chief grinned as though pleased with himself. He pulled open his desk draw and rummaged around for a couple of seconds. 'Here it is.' He pulled out a brown envelope and tossed it across the desk to his son. Matthews ripped it open and poured the contents out onto his hand; it was a large metal key. Matthews looked back quizzical.

'You remember your grandmother's old house on the west cliff, quite a lovely terraced house with the great views of the sea and abbey?'

'Of course, I spent more time in that house than my own as a kid.'

'Well when she passed last year the house became your mother's ownership and she never knew what to do with it. We had told Charlotte she could move into it when she gets married, but knowing your sister it will end up empty for years, whilst she waits for prince fucking charming to show up, and your brother Robert already has a house with his wife in Ruswarp. We had thought about renting it out but the place is full of your grandmothers belongings, we haven't had time to clear it yet. So it's perfect for you.' His father grinned, Matthews on the other hand was not. He loved his grandmother dearly, but even when she was alive the house was a complete mess, she had died over six months ago and his thoughts on how the house would look now were not pretty.

'Fine, I will go take a look at it and unpack, there is still enough hours in the day to get anything I may need from the shops.' He stood to leave.

'Hold on son, I haven't even told you the best news yet. Sit, sit.' Matthews did as he was told. The chief then slid across another brown envelope across the desk, and gestured for his son to take it.

'What is this?' Matthews took it, but did not open it.

'Your first case.'

'I beg your pardon?'

'This morning a body was discovered on the beach.' The chief shifted in his chair and cleared his throat with a deep cough. 'Not a stone's throw from that new pavilion on the cliffside. I was called there this morning and have written up a report of what could be seen, I was able to get a sketch drawing of how the body was laid on the sand, which I know sounds odd but it will become clear when you see it. In the envelope you'll find my report, the sketch, plus details of the gentleman who discovered the body during his morning dog walk. I have also written down the details of where the body has been taken, you will probably want to get over and see it as soon as possible.'

'But surely this is not the job of a constable, haven't you got one of the inspectors on this…oh I see…' Matthews threw the envelope back onto the desk, 'you are signing me up to partner one of them, who is it? Please tell me it's not Andrew Suggitt, I don't know how he ever made inspector. Thicker than duck shit if you ask me.'

'No, I am not partnering you up. This is what I have been trying to tell you since you walked in. I didn't transfer you to Whitby to continue being a PC, I am hiring you as a DC, detective constable.' Matthews stood again, his mouth open in shock.

'But there is no such rank as a DC?'

'True, most detectives are private and not associated with the police station, but I know this is what you ultimately want to be.'

'You can't just make up a position for me!'

'Actually I can, this is my station and I can call

you the fucking tooth fairy if I want to.' He grinned at his own sarcasm but Matthews did not. 'See it this way, you get to be a detective and I get to have a detective working closely with the station, instead of against it like they usually do. You can have an office here that you can use as much or as little as you want, we would just require you to check in with reports of what you're investigating on a regular basis.'

'No, no, no. I told you I didn't want special treatment for being the chief's son.' His voice was raising again. 'I told you this is why I wanted to stay in York. What are the other officers going to think me just walking in here and getting such a promotion? No, I'm sorry father but I can't do that.' He turned his back on his father and stormed out of the office, snatching his suitcase on his way. The chief bolted from his chair at lightning speed, snatched the envelope and followed. He ran out of the door and seized his son by the arm right in front of the secretaries desk.

'I need a good detective in this town, and I know your performance in York has been incredible, you have intuition second to none. You can distance yourself emotionally from crime, and more importantly you see things that many officers miss. Yes, I wanted you in Whitby for selfish personal reasons, but I also wanted you because you are proving to be a bloody incredible officer, and I certainly could do with one here. Now take the blasted envelope and get on with it, I want to see you tomorrow afternoon with an update.'

With that he returned to his office before his son could protest further and slammed the door. Matthews stood there for a moment in silence, what on earth just happened?

CHAPTER 3

Matthews left the police station in a fluster, kicking the railings outside as he passed. With his suitcase in one hand, and the envelope containing the investigation information in the other he checked his coat pocket to make sure he had the key to his grandmother's house. It was there, which was a relief as it meant he didn't have to go back into his father's office. Although he knew it was not in ideal place to live, he was more thinking about how unkept it was likely to be, he knew it would be much better than being under the same roof as his father. He turned back to face the grand station building and rolled his eyes with a loud sigh, having his father as his boss was his worst nightmare, and it just became his reality.

'Detective Matthews?' a quiet voice called from the doorway, Matthews was a little taken aback at being called detective, especially given that he had only found out himself only seconds ago. A teenage boy, about fourteen years old, exited the police station. He approached Matthews with an extended hand. 'Pleased to meet you sir, my name is Harvey, I'm one of the stable hands and carriage drivers. Chief asked me to drive ya around today. He tells me that if I do good helpin' ya with stuff he may consider me for trainin'. I've always wanted to be a police officer ya see.' He was a tall skinny lad with a pale complexion which was covered in a layer of dirt. He had a thick head of brown messy hair and sleepy looking dark eyes, yet his smile was warm and sincere.

'Has he now...' Matthews was going to dismiss the young lad, but remembering he mentioned being his carriage driver anywhere, decided a lift to the house was not a bad idea. 'Where is the carriage?'

'Just wait here sir, I'll bring it around front.' With

that he shot off as fast as he could around the building and out of sight. Matthews laid the suitcase on the ground and looked at the door key still in his hand, his thoughts flooded with memories of his grandmother. He remembered how she was always in her kitchen baking pies and breads; it was the only part of her house he really had memories of her in. As a young boy Matthews loved the smell of his grandmothers cooking and would often help, she was particularly good at cooking a Sunday roast, and her Yorkshire puddings were the highlight in Matthews opinion. He didn't know how he felt about moving into her old house, he had been there almost every day before he had left Whitby, and he hadn't been back to her house since she had died. It was certainly going to be an odd experience returning after all this time.

A minute later Harvey returned guiding two beautiful black horses, they were pulling a small carriage. 'Woah boys.' He patted the one nearest to him as he brought them to a stop in front of Detective Matthews. 'Allow me sir.' he took the suitcase from the ground and carried it around to the back of the carriage where he secured it in place, he then returned to open the door for Matthews to get inside. 'Where to sir?'

Matthews looked at the key he still held in his hand, and the envelope in his other. Today was Thursday and he hadn't expected to be given a case by his father for a couple of days, how wrong he was to think such a thing.

'I need to speak with the coroner, and then I'll need to make a stop off for some groceries before heading home. Do you need to be back at the station by a certain time?'

'Nah, chief said I've to assist you today for as long as I'm needed.' Harvey's voice never seemed to raise very loud when he spoke and Matthews sometimes had to concentrate more than usual to make sure he didn't miss what he was saying.

'I see.' Matthews knew the young lad would know his connection to the chief. 'Well let us get on then.' Harvey slammed the door shut and took his seat upfront, his voice barely audible from the carriage as he instructed the horses to go.

The carriage was not the most comfortable of

places, and smelt of damp and sweaty feet. The wooden bench he sat upon had only a thin blanket covering it, which gave no cushioning to the rider. The windows of the doors, one at each side, did not have a cover over them so he watched as he passed by the train station and made their way into town. Matthews had always loved the sound of horse hoofs along the road, he had been a regular visitor of the police stables as a youngster. One of his school friends had worked there for a short time and so Matthews would join him grooming and cleaning out.

As they passed through town, Matthews couldn't help but think how the place never seemed to change. The River Esk, which flowed through the centre of the town was lined with hundreds of fishing boats of all sizes, and workers of all different ages could be seen from dusk 'til dawn unloading the latest catch and restocking the boats ready for the next sailing. Whitby was a thriving fishing town, and most people either worked on the harbour or had family members who did.

The journey to the coroner was short, and once

outside Matthews knocked on the door. The doorway was up a narrow ally, which could not fit the horse and cart, so he had to walk up the final few yards alone; the building itself was hidden from the main street. The alley didn't lead anywhere and came to an end at the coroner's door. With the envelope of information in hand he waited for an answer, and after a few seconds the sound of keys scrabbling behind the door could be heard, and moments later an elderly man appeared around the doorframe.

'Can I help you?' The man's voice croaked.

'Ah, yes…my name is…' He paused for a moment, suddenly realising his new title. 'Detective Matthews. I have been given the case regarding the man found on the beach this morning and was wondering if I could speak to you about him.'

'I've been expecting ya.' The old man opened up the door and beckoned for the detective to come inside. 'Mr Waters at your service.' He held out an extended hand to the detective who immediately returned the handshake. 'You are here just in time actually, I've just hung up the photographs in the dark room. I imagine they should be ready in a moment.'

'Photographs?' Matthews quizzed.

'Ey, I set up a dark room last year, got myself a cracking camera to take pictures of bodies at the scene. Although it's a bloody big thing to carry. Can sometimes come in handy for documenting autopsies too, especially if there's a hearing and they want evidence to look at, marvellous bit of equipment if you ask me. Follow me.' He slammed the door shut and locked it before guiding the detective through the building. They eventually came to a room lit by a single candle cased in a fancy red glass shade. The room was small with a worktop running along the back wall, above which two washing lines hung with pieces of paper clipped to them.

'Did you manage to take many pictures on the beach Mr Waters?' He watched as the elderly man inspected the hanging papers.

'Just a couple, I got there just as they were about to move him, so I took some before bringing him back here for examination. Here we are.' He unclipped one of the photographs, which Detective Matthews could not see anything on due to the poor lighting. 'Oh that's a shame, this one didn't work. Let's see if the others have come out.' He took down a further two photographs and held them both closer to the light. 'Ah, yes, you see here look.' Matthews came in closer and gasped when his eyes focused on the photographs. One showed the man from the waist up, his arms raised above his head as he lay on the ground. The second picture was of the man's face, and his hands above with his wrists and neck tied onto a strange structure.

'What in God's name?' the detective cursed.

'Do you want to see the body detective? I've got that wooden structure that he was tied to as well, thought you may wish to see it.' Mr Waters handed the photographs to the detective who placed them inside his envelope.

'Yes please, just a quick look. Have you examined him yet?'

'I haven't opened him up yet, but I have stripped

him of his clothes and started documenting the external examinations.' He guided the detective back along the corridor and into a much larger room with bright natural light coming from an overhead window. The whole building reeked of death and a chemical odour that Matthews couldn't identify. 'He has some bruises to the upper arms, and of course the wrists are badly cut due to them being tied up.' Mr Waters pulled back the sheet, which covered the dead man's body, uncovering him only to the waist.

Matthews had seen dead bodies before; it was an occupational expectation, so he was less than distressed at seeing this pale lifeless man rested on the table like a slab of meat. The bruises on his arms could be seen clearly, an indication of a struggle perhaps, and the cuts on his wrists from the object, which had been tied to him, looked raw and sore. His skin was dried from the salt water, with his lips and eyelids the worse effected. He was a tall man, muscular and in appearance seemed to be in good physical health. His naked torso did not show any signs of bruises or marks.

'Are the injuries on his arms the only marks you

have found?' Matthews asked, hoping he wouldn't move the cover even further to reveal the man's private area.

'No, I haven't seen any other marks I think are of concern.'

'Do you think he died from drowning or was he put there dead before the tide came in?'

'Difficult to say without opening him up. But looking at his build and the small restraints I can't see him just lying there as the tide consumed him.'

'Agreed. Do we have an ID on him?'

'He didn't have anything on him that I can identify him with, and none of the officers or the man who found him knew who he was either.'

'Thank you for your time Mr Waters. Once your report is ready please send it to the police station for me to go through.' He shook the senior man's hand and showed himself out.

Matthews returned to the main street where he could see Harvey returning from up the street. He had sent the young lad on errands to collect him some groceries; he knew it wasn't really his job but he thought it would keep him occupied whilst he waited. The cobbled Church street was filled with people of all ages going about their business, and Matthews couldn't help but smile. He may begrudge his return to Whitby, but he certainly did love the town.

'Sorry for keeping ya waiting detective, I stopped at the troughs for the horses to have a drink before heading back.' He opened the carriage door for him as he spoke.

'No problem young man, I have only just left.'

'Where to now sir?'

'Home I think.'

'Erm…sorry, sir. I'm not sure where that is?' Harvey questioned with an air of embarrassment. Matthews laughed, realising his lack of details and instructed the young lad accordingly.

The journey back across town was again a short one, and the climb up the steep road to the top of west cliff saw Harvey dismount his seat and guide the horses slowly. Most of the streets in Whitby were a dirt track, and so the horse's hooves would sometimes have less grip on the steep inclines.

When the carriage pulled up outside his grandmother's old house Matthews couldn't wipe the smile from his face. He had only good memories in this house. Harvey opened the carriage and Matthews went to unlock the front door, leaving Harvey to bring the suitcase. The door creaked open and the smell of dust and damp flooded Detective Matthews nostrils. He stepped over the threshold and took in the sight of the hallway and staircase. His grandmother had died over six months ago, and looking at the condition and smell of the house, nobody had been in to clean up since.

CHAPTER 4

Matthews spent the remained of the evening making a start cleaning the house; it was certainly going to be a lengthy procedure. He couldn't quite believe that he was now living in his grandmother's old house. Cobwebs hung in every room, the intricate, delicate, sculpture of silky white thread undisturbed for so long that they covered the walls and ceiling in grey dusty clumps. The abandoned house looked more like a Halloween horror house than a warm welcoming home. The carpets and furniture were layered with a thick coat of dust; and the water from the kitchen sink run brown for the first couple of minutes. Cleaning this house would take days, and Matthews was already exhausted before he had even begun.

At nine o'clock there was a knock on the door. Matthews could see his father through the living room window. Matthews groaned, he had hoped he could avoid him for a day or two until he felt ready to speak to him again. He was still angry with him and didn't wish to argue again at this late hour. He opened the door and before he could say anything his father pushed his way in.

'Settling in are we?' His voice echoed through the house. It was only then that Matthews realised how quiet it had been before his arrival. 'Brought you these over, figured you wouldn't have time to do laundry with whatever is here.' He handed him some fresh bedding and towels. 'You can keep them, you know how many your mother had, and I don't need them now. Blimey it's worse in here than I thought it would be, but it'll be grand once it's had a clean-up.'

'Do you want to stay for a drink?' Matthews asked. 'I'm afraid I don't have much at the moment.'

'No, it's ok. Have you eaten?' his father asked whilst rummaging through a large shopping bag. 'Your sister made you some pie, figured you wouldn't have eaten, she's a worrier just like your mother, and a feeder too.' He chuckled as he handed over a ceramic plate covered with a small cloth.

'Oh, yes, thank you.' He could still feel the warmth of the food on the bottom of the plate.

'Let me know if I can get you anything. Probably in need of a sprucing up in here, will take a bit of time of course but it's a grand old house really. Just let me know what you need and I'll have it sent through.' He gave a forced smile and there was an awkward silence for barely a second before he turned and headed back towards the door.

'By the way Pops, Mr Waters gave me some of the pictures he took on the beach this morning. I'll make a start looking into all that tomorrow morning.'

'That's a boy. It's good to have you on the force. I've asked young Harvey to call for you in the morning. He's switched on that young lad, could learn a thing or two under your supervision.'

'I don't need somebody to babysit,' Matthews said.

'I don't know too much about him, he's been in the yard now a couple of years and shows he has a good head on his shoulders, wants to be an officer one day and if he shows promise I may consider it. Anyway, don't consider it babysitting; consider it somebody to help with the heavy lifting. Good night.' With that he let himself out. The large heavy wooden door slammed loudly causing the dust of the cobwebs above to fall along the hallway.

Matthews returned to the kitchen and turned on the gas to the hob and struck a match to light it. He placed an old copper kettle on to boil and whilst waiting for it to heat, he unwrapped the food from his sister. It was a chicken and ham pie, and no sooner had he uncovered it had he unceremoniously picked up the still warm pie to eat; his first meal since breakfast.

He found an old small tray which he used to

carry a pot of tea and a China plate decorated in blue and white patterns, upon which he had placed a couple of biscuits purchased that afternoon in town. He took the tray through to the living room and placed it onto the coffee table next to the envelope containing the investigation information he had yet to look through. As he landed on the sofa with an exhausted thud a cloud of dust consumed him. He coughed waving his hands in front of his face to help clear the dust. He made sure his tray was dust free, and then poured the tea into a China cup and dunked one of his biscuits before lighting a cigarette.

The envelope on the table containing his newly assigned case filled him with dread, not because of the case itself, which he knew very little about, but because he knew that once he inspected the envelope the realisation he was staying in Whitby would become ever more real.

He finished his cigarette, drunk the last of his tea and lit a couple more candles to brighten up the darkening room. The envelope was not thick or heavy, which basically meant there was very little known about the case already. Inside was the two photographs given to him by Mr Waters, which he stared at for a couple of seconds in disbelief. The only other item in the envelope was a one sided piece of paper written in his father's hand. It stated the date, the time of which the body was discovered, the name and address of the man who found it, and an estimated time of death which had next to it '(*to be confirmed by coroner*)'.

'Well this is hardly a lot to go with.' Matthews sighed before returning to the kitchen to boil the kettle again so he could prepare a bath. It too needed cleaning first before he could use it, and after thirty minutes of cleaning the bathroom he had given up and decided to instead just wash and get himself ready for bed. His grandmothers old double bed however was much worse, the bedding his father had giving him was perfect, but the mattress he laid it on was covered in mould and it was another thirty minutes of cleaning and beating off the dust before he could make it up for sleeping. He didn't sleep well at all that night, and despite his murder investigation he knew the first thing he was going to do the next day was get a new bed.

***

Matthews had been awake for an hour when Harvey knocked on the door at precisely eight o'clock.

'G'morning sir,' Harvey's enthusiastic voice rung out, 'I've got something for you.' He handed the detective a small bag which was sealed. 'Was left at the station last night for you from Mr Waters, says it was what he found in the stiff's trouser pocket.'

'Thank you, Harvey, but please don't refer to him as a "stiff". Come on inside a moment so I can have a closer look.' He guided the young lad back into his house and towards the kitchen. He unsealed the bag and carefully tipped its contents out onto the table.

'What is it?' Harvey asked, screwing up his face as he stared at the unidentifiable item.

'That I believe is a piece of paper,' he pointed at the water damaged paper, 'that there I'd say is a one-pound note, you can kind of make out the ink on it,' Harvey nodded but wasn't sure he could really see it in the soggy pile. 'And there maybe something else too; it's difficult to say as it's all mushed together due to the sea water. Clearly he had all these items in the same pocket.' They both leant over the items with intrigue. 'Let's see if we can un-prise any of it and get any ideas of who he is.' Harvey watched in awe as Matthews used two folks to carefully unravel the mangled mess, it was clear straight away that paper money was indeed entangled with other paper. Harvey leaned in closer, and using his little finger tried to assist the detective in prising apart the mushed paper, unsure if he was really helping at all.

'Wait, what is that.' He hollered at quite a volume, causing the detective to jump. 'Sorry.' He quickly said realising his rather dramatic squeal.

'I think I saw what you did,' the detective said as he returned to the section. 'Ah, yes. Can you see that?' It was the corner of what looked like a logo stamped onto the piece of paper, it was blue inked and was difficult to tell for certain what the entire logo could be. 'Looking at the paper I think this stamp was at the top of the page, maybe even top middle, so it could be a logo or company brand. A lot of businesses like to stamp letters or documents as it makes them appear more official.'

'Can you tell what it's from?'

'Unfortunately, far too much has been washed away. But let's put it to the side and keep digging through the mess, we may get another clue.'

The detective placed the potential logo to one side for safety, and continued with care to search through the distorted mess of paper with Harvey. They were about to give up when another clue presented itself.

'Look!' shouted Harvey, 'that bit there has something written on it.' Matthews had spotted it too and carefully prised the delicate paper away from the mass. The letters on the torn paper were smudged and the words could barely be read.

'I wonder if this is written in the victim's hand?' Matthews wondered aloud.

'H…loc…ace.' Harvey spoke aloud, trying to figure out the blanks. 'Wait, it could be Havelock Place, it's a street not too far from here.' He looked at Matthews with a wide grin on his face. Matthews pulled the paper in for a closer look and beamed back at him.

'Well done Harvey, that certainly could be it.'

The street name was written on different paper to the stamp, and frustratingly the house number was completely destroyed. 'Where have I heard that before?' Matthews tapped his fingers on the table as he tried to recall why that street name rang familiar. 'Hold on a minute.' He crossed the kitchen and reached for the envelope his father had given him, and pulled out the single paged report he had been given. He scanned his eyes over it and there in his fathers handwriting was the street name Havelock Place. It was the exact same street name as given by the witness who found the body, as his contact address.

CHAPTER 5

etective Matthews placed his father's written report, the photographs and a fresh notepad and pencils into his small thin leather briefcase before leaving the house. Harvey rushed ahead to open the carriage door for the detective, and nearly crashed into it he was running so fast.

Matthews thanked him for opening the door for him as he stepped inside. As Harvey closed the door and rushed up to the horse Matthews leaned out of the window to speak to him.

'Harvey,' he called, and the young lad immediately spun around to see, 'let's go the long way to Havelock Place and go via the cliff tops so I can see the beach where he was found. We don't need to stop I'll just look from the carriage this time, I just want to get an idea how far away the body was to the closest houses.

They passed over the cliffside in the carriage only a couple of minutes later, and Matthews leaned out of the carriage window as they slowed down. There was obviously nothing to see other than the beach, and the houses set back against the cliff were so far back that they were unlikely to see anything happening down on the beach, the cliffs were just too high. There was however the pavilion building which was built hanging over the cliff edge. He made a note to himself to pay them a visit later as Harvey swung the carriage to the left and away from the sea front.

Havelock Place was lined on both sides with tall terraced town houses. On one side they were all grand red bricked houses, with stones steps leading up to the front door. On the opposite side of the street the houses were much larger and were white washed giving them a more grandeur appearance.

Matthews dismounted the carriage and walked along the street until he came to the house he needed, it was one of the red brick ones. He climbed the small couple of steps and as he knocked on the large wooden door, a voice came from behind startling him.

'May I help you?' Ernest O'Sullivan was returning home from walking his King Charles spaniel.

'Mr O'Sullivan is it? My name is PC...I mean, Detective Matthews. I have taken on the case regarding the man you found on the beach yesterday morning, and wondered if I could ask you a couple of questions?'

'Sure,' said Ernest in his gruff voice, 'but don't be expecting much more information cos I don't know nuffin'.' He unlocked the front door and showed the detective into the living room, it had the odour of tobacco smoke and the brown seating and yellowing walls did little to disguise it. 'Just wrong place wrong time, as they say. Take a seat detective; I'll just take Molly here into the kitchen. Would you like a drink or anything?'

'No thank you.' Matthews took a seat on the long sofa, leaving the armchair, which looked as though it was Mr O'Sullivan's favourite chair given how flat the cushion on it was. The living room was quite modest in size, and had minimal furniture, there was an open fire that was currently lifeless, although a barrel of coal sat beside it ready to be used. The fire wasn't lit but the halve was dusted in white ash from the night before. A large wooden cabinet lined the back wall, and it was filled with picture frames of all different shapes and sizes, each one displaying a different member of the family. There was also a collection of porcelain ornaments lining the fire place and windowsill.

'So detective,' Mr O'Sullivan grunted as he returned, landing hard into the arm chair, 'what questions do you need to know?'

'Mr O'Sullivan, I have some information that you gave the chief regarding the time you found the body in the morning, but I was wondering if you took your dog for a walk late on an evening the same way, and if so did you see anything?'

'To be honest lad, it's all about if the tide is in or

not, and how light it is. If it's in, I'll walk along the cliff top. I normally take Molly for a final walk around ten thirty, but I don't take her as far as in the morning. It's normally dark by then so I wouldn't go down on the beach that late. I don't recall seeing anything though.'

'Tell me, although you say you don't know the man, have you seen him around the town before?'

'Goodness me lad, there's thousands that live and work in Whitby, I can't remember everyone.' Mr O'Sullivan gave a throaty cough before continuing. 'No detective, I don't have any awareness of seeing him before. He ain't from around this part of town as I'd more likely of seen him.'

'As you can imagine he didn't have any identification on him, so I will begin making enquiries around the town. I would appreciate it if you let me know if you hear anything.'

'Certainly detective. You know what folk are like round 'ere, nothings secret. Whole bloody towns probably heard about it by now.'

'Can I ask you Mr O'Sullivan what it is you do

for a living?'

'Retired. Army man in my youth.' His voice was coarse and cold.

'Have you lived in Whitby your entire life?' Matthews made small notes about the man as he spoke.

'Mother was from Whitby, she moved inland to Pickering when she married my father, but after he died she returned here. I was off in the army and when I left I came to Whitby to take care of her; got myself a job as a coast guard manager until I retired myself.'

'Do you live here alone?'

'My wife, Elizabeth, has gone to the market. She should be home soon. Then there is Molly the dog of course. Will you need to speak with the wife?'

'I shouldn't think that be necessary. One more thing before I go Mr O'Sullivan.' Matthews stood to leave, Mr O'Sullivan followed him to the door. 'In the pocket of the victim was some papers, mostly destroyed due to the sea water, but I have been able to identify a couple of things that I'm hopeful will help towards identifying the man. One of which was a street name, and the reason needed to see you again was because the street name was Havelock Place.' Mr O'Sullivan's face dropped. For the first time he looked genuinely concerned.

'Ah, I see…yes well that looks even worse for me doesn't it.'

'It may be a coincidence of course. Whitby is not that large of a place, but I need to figure out if he was maybe visiting somebody or looking for lodgings.'

'There is nobody on this street that runs a guesthouse, not unless it's somebody that was going to let him stay because they knew him. But then how'd you end up dead like that if he only just arrived in town?'

'Thank you for your time Mr O'Sullivan, I will most likely be in touch again.' Matthews shook Mr O'Sullivan's hand and bid him farewell.

Outside Harvey was waiting with the horses, 'Where too now, sir?'

'I think before we go to the station I would like to just drop in at the pavilion, since we are so close to it. You never know, somebody there might have seen something.'

'Right you are, sir.' Harvey gave a salute as he turned back to the horses. The Pavilion too was walking distance, and Matthews felt this was somewhat stretching the need, but it seemed to be pleasing Harvey to be of assistance.

Chapter 6

They arrived at the Pavilion within minutes. From the road side the building could have almost been missed. It was build down the rock face so low that only a slither of roofline was visible to the street above. Matthews left Harvey and the carriage by the side of the road and took the stone staircase down towards the entrance.

The Pavilion was a redbrick building with white painted stone framing the windows and a slate roof. The entrance was at the side of the building, which from this angle was only three floors high and four large windows wide. It looked more like a grand house than a theatre. However, despite this the building stretched along the cliff face quite a considerable amount, making it longer than Tate Hill pier.

The theatre was not yet open today, and so Matthews simply knocked on the door and waited to see if there was any response. After a couple of seconds, a man came to the door.

'Can I help you?' he asked, his voice nasal. He was of average height yet extremely skinny with dark hair and deep-set sleepy eyes that had large bags under them. He looked to be in his early thirties, wore black boots, grey trousers and a dark shirt.

'My name is constab... erm ... Detective Matthews and I am here...'

'Oh, I wondered when I'd be seeing one of your lot,' the man interrupted, 'come in.'

'Thank you.' Matthews wasn't sure he appreciated the rudeness of this man, but regardless he followed him through to a small office area just beside the doorway.

'Take a seat detective.' The man gestured towards a shabby wooden chair before taking his own seat behind a rather small and somewhat littered desk.

'Could I get your name please?' Matthews asked whilst retrieving his note pad and pencil from his bag.

'Names William, you can call me Will for short. I'm one of the security men at the Pavilion. In fact, you just caught me as I'm about to leave.'

'I see, I will try and make this quick then. You said that you had been expecting one of my lot. Can you tell me why?'

'Well the body on the beach yesterday morning of course, been expecting one of you to come around asking questions.'

'Can I ask how you know about the body?'

'Saw it being taken away, will no doubt be in the gazette this morning too.'

'May I ask what hours were you working yesterday and the day before?'

'Do the same hours all the time. I start at ten, roughly the time the punters are being kicked out, and I go through to nine or ten the next morning.'

'You said you were *one* of the security men that worked here, can you tell me the others?'

'Just me and Edward, he just left. But to be honest he's an old fart that can barely deal with locking up anymore, I don't know why they keep him. Put on a load of weight since I started too and can barely even handle the stairs anymore.'

'When is it you started working here?'

'Oh about six months ago, maybe a little longer.'

'And you both do the night shift?'

'Yes. The boss should be here any minute and then he and the staff look after the place during the day, us security just man the place at night.' He gave a yawn and looked less than impressed at being kept from going home.

'When you arrived at work on Wednesday night was it already completely dark, or could you see out onto the beach at all.'

'Let me stop you there detective.' He raised his hand as he said this. 'When I get here I ain't looking at the beach, it's all about ensuring everybody has left and the building is locked down. The staff leaves not long afterwards and by midnight it's usually just myself and Edward left.' His tone was getting more and more rude.

'So what about in the morning?' Matthews was becoming inpatient with the man already. 'You must have seen something given you were expecting me.'

'I just saw a cluster of people on the beach, it caught my attention given it was early. I realised it was the chief of police with a handful of others, and it wasn't long before a stretcher came to move a body. It doesn't take a genius to work out what must have happened. Daft fool probably got pissed and drowned.'

'So the group of people standing on the beach was the first time you noticed anything?'

'Yeah. I do a walk around every hour or so, and the tide was in on my last check so yes that was the first I saw; not that looking out onto the beach is my usual routine. They were using the steps further along the cliff, so none of them even came past the Pavilion windows.'

'Do you ever get people wandering past the Pavilion on a night, since there's a pathway down to the beach here too?'

'On occasion, the coloured beach huts are at the bottom of the path here so it's usually people going to them. But I can't say I saw anybody that night.' He sighed. 'Do you need anything else or can I go home now?'

'I think that is all for now. If I need any more from you or your co-workers I will call back. If you don't think there is anything else I need to know then I will let myself out.'

'You not want to see the boss?'

'Not right now, although I may come back.' Detective Matthews let himself out of the office and William escorted him back to the front door.

'If you ask me detective it was probably a drunken fight gone too far.'

Matthews politely wished the man a pleasant day and made his way back to Harvey and the carriage. Back on top of the cliff Matthews paused and looked onwards to where the next set of stairs was located. It seemed quite a distance, so it is plausible he didn't see much until he was purposefully looking that way.

Back up on the street stood Harvey and the horse drawn carriage. Harvey clearly hadn't realised Matthews was approaching as he stood talking to his horses without a care in the world. Matthews cleared his throat to alert him of his arrival, and Harvey blushed with embarrassment.

'To the station now, sir?' Harvey jumped to attention and opened up the carriage door for the detective. Matthews laughed, he found the boy rather amusing and the company was proving to be valued after all.

'Yes, let's head to the station, I need to speak to all residents on Havelock Place but will see if there are any spare hands available to lighten the weight; it'll take days to work through every house alone.' Harvey nodded and closed the carriage door after the detective, and proceeded with guiding the horses away.

As the carriage drove along Matthews made final notes of his conversation with Mr O'Sullivan, and even made some from the pavilion. Mr O'Sullivan seemed an unlikely suspect, Matthews thought, but as it stood he was the only one he had.

The noise of the town centre came into ear shot and Matthews watched from the carriage window as the buildings and houses passed by. Despite this his mind was not on the town at all. He was thinking about the transfer his father put in on his behalf, and wondered if he could do the same to return to York, once this case he had been given was complete.

His attention was soon caught however as they passed an open doorway, and Grace, the woman from the train, walked out. She didn't notice the detective, who rode by in the carriage, but turned back to her fiancé who followed her out of the door. Their voices were raised and Matthews gasped with horror when he saw the man slap Grace around the face, causing her to scream and fall to the ground.

'Stop the carriage,' he shouted up the Harvey, and leaned out of the window to open the door for himself. He jumped out into the road before the carriage had fully stopped, managing to stay on his feet by a mere coincidence. He raced over to Grace's side and quickly took her elbow to assist her to her feet. Grace jumped with fright, pulling her arm away with force before realising who had come to her aid. She gave a soft, almost embarrassed smile to the detective as he helped her to her feet.

'Who the fuck are you?' the fiancé snarled in anger, squaring up to the detective and forcing his hand from Graces elbow.

'I am Detective Matthews of the Whitby police, and…'

'Please detective,' Grace cut in, 'all is well here, you may leave us.'

'Miss I cannot walk away if I think you are in danger.'

'Thank you detective, I appreciate your concern; but there is nothing to worry about here.' She gave him a long hard stare. 'Please detective.'

Grace walked back to her fiancé side in the doorway, Matthews didn't want to leave her with this brute of a man, but he had no choice. He returned to the carriage, looking back occasionally at Grace who remained in the arms of her fiancé, who was grinning with satisfaction at the detectives failed intervention. Matthews watched as Grace returned inside her house as Harvey drove the carriage away. Just before they were about to leave the harbour and head up towards the police station detective Matthews once again called for the carriage to be stopped.

'Is everything okay, sir?' Harvey dismounted from the driver's seat and leaned into the carriage doors open window. Inside the detective was rummaging through his briefcase and pulled the small sealed bag containing the mangled pieces of paper. Carefully he removed a piece and joined Harvey on the side of the road, looking back along the river side he scanned the various fishing docks.

'Look at that,' he said to Harvey, holding up the piece of paper to eye level. Harvey tried to see exactly where his gaze was pointing. 'What do you think? They look the same right?'

Against one of the unloading bay fences was a large logo, it was a simple blue square with an even more simple outline of a fish inside. The paper in Matthews hand showed the corner of the square and the nose of the fish. On the loading bay fence, underneath the logo was the company name, Ocean Venture.

'You think it's that?' Harvey asked.

'Well there is only one way to find out. Park the horses over there and follow me.' Harvey did as he was told and tied the horses up outside one of the public houses, before racing after the detective who had gone on ahead.

CHAPTER 7

By the time Harvey had caught up, Detective Matthews had already spoken to a young boy, a couple of years younger than Harvey, who ran off just as Harvey approached. He had gone to fetch the dock manager as requested to him by Matthews. The pair of them stood just outside the loading bay, and watched the multitude of men unloading the large fishing boats that had recently docked.

The river Esk was lined with many docking areas, and boats of all sizes were being loaded and unloaded along the harbour constantly throughout the day. Hundreds of men and boys worked here and with the number of fishing vestals there was always work to be done. The detective could barely hear his own thoughts over the sound of crates be thrown around and the sound of men's voices shouting over one and other to be heard. It was certainly a different type of hustle and bustle to that of York, thought Matthews. It also had a very different smell, one which Matthews could only stomach for so long before having to leave.

'Detective, I hear you wish to speak with me?' A large man with a thick bushy black beard, and wearing dungarees approached Matthews and Harvey, he held out a hand which the detective immediately shook. At first glance Harvey thought he looked like a pirate. His voice was croaky and the skin on his face and hands were flaking slightly due to the salty sea water drying it out.

'Are you the manager of the Ocean Venture fleet?'

'That'll be me. Names Brown, Peter Brown.' He strained his voice over the surrounding noise and struggling to raise his clearly straining voice any further said, 'Why don't we head on over to my office where it's a little quieter?'

He guided the detective across the road and through a small doorway nestled between two shop fronts; any passer-by would have walked past this door without even noticing it due to it being so plain and inconspicuous. Harvey waited outside where he could keep watch of his horses that were parked up a couple of doors along the street.

The office was no bigger than a broom cupboard, but managed to squeeze in a small desk with a chair at both sides. There were maps of the sea surrounding Whitby on the wall and two paintings, one of a fishing boat out in the harbour, and the second of a man who Matthews predicted was a relative of Peter Brown.

'Please, take a seat detective.' Matthews sat on the wonky old wooden chair opposite Mr Brown, the room smelt of seaweed.

'Thank you for your time Mr Brown, I won't keep you long.'

'Good, I've got six boats to unload. Now what can I do for you detective?'

Matthews pulled out of his briefcase the small mushed up paper with the corner of a logo showing, and placed it on the desk. Mr Brown looked slightly confused by this but waited for the detective to explain himself.

'Mr Brown, yesterday morning a man was found dead on the beach. We believe it to have been murder. However, we have yet to figure out the identity of this man.' Mr Brown's heavy expression softened to concern. 'In his pocket we found traces of papers, mostly unreadable due to the sea water, however this piece here looks as though it should be a stamp, or logo. As I passed your dock just now it looks similar to the logo on your sign.'

'Ey, yes I can see that too. But I don't know anything about a body.' He looked nervous as though he was being accused.

'Mr Brown, I have a photograph in my bag of the body, it shows the face quite well. Would you be willing to take a look to see if you recognise him?'

'Sure,' said Mr Brown. Detective Matthews slid across one of the pictures. Mr Brown gasped with horror. 'What the fuck…yes I do recognise him, but what the hell is he tied to?'

'That I am not sure. Was he an employee of yours?'

'Yes, never on the boats, just on the loading bay, he had muscle to help unload the heavy crates. I feel bad now cos I was calling him all kinds of names this morning for not turning up.'

'Could you tell me his name?'

'James…er…Shit what's his last name.' Mr Brown began tapping his forehead as he racked his brain to think of the man's surname. 'Fuck, I can't remember his last name. I don't usually need to remember.'

'How long was he in employment with you Mr Brown?'

'Not long. To be quite honest it's only the boat crew we have on the books, any hands in the loading bay are paid for a day's work as and when they show up. We have the regulars who come most days, and then we have the strays who come and go.

James was here most days, he's not from Whitby but has been in town, I'd say just over six, seven months, something like that. If you wait here detective I'll see if David Turner is around, he knows more about James than I do, I think they go drinking together.'

Mr Brown left the office, leaving the detective alone. This gave him a couple of minutes to write in his note book before Mr Brown returned with a younger man in his mid-thirties.

'Do you need me to stay Detective?' Mr Brown asked, already half way through the door.

'Not right now Mr Brown but I may need to come back sometime if that's okay.'

'Perfectly, now if you'll excuse me I am needed on the bay.'

He exited, leaving the detective with the young man who took the seat across the desk occupied by his boss just minutes ago.

'Detective, Mr Brown tells me this is about James.' David Turner was a thin man with short curly hair and wore filthy overalls that looked as though they were covered in fish guts. His voice was deep and articulate which did not match his appearance at all. The detective showed Mr Turner the same photograph of the body on the beach.

'Can you confirm this is him?'

'Woah… yes that's him.' He couldn't look at the picture for more than a second and pushed it back to the detective. 'What happened to him?'

'Mr Turner do you know James' surname by any chance?'

'Yes sir, it's Robinson.' Detective Matthews kept his notebook out and continued to make notes.

'Do you know where he has been staying?'

'He's been renting a room on Church Street. The guest house owned by Mrs Sheppard, crazy old bat, you've probably heard of her.' Mr Turner snorted.

'Tell me, how long has Mr Robinson been staying at the guesthouse?'

'Oh I'm not sure, probably the whole time. He's

only been here in Whitby less than a year. I told him it'd be cheaper to get a room somewhere else, but he seemed keen to stay there.'

'Would you consider Mr Robinson a friend, did you socialise outside work?'

'Oh yes, not every day, but we would sometimes have a pint or two in the Black Horse. Was one of the only pubs which let him in anymore, he was barred from quite a few.'

'Really? Why?'

'Fighting mostly, he had a temper on him. Certainly didn't have any friends that's for sure, even I wouldn't consider myself that close to him. He got kicked out of the Duke of York once for harassing the waitress, putting his hand up her skirt he was. The White Horse and Griffin banned him for trashing the place, after getting so drunk he started throwing chairs. It was rare you'd see him with anyone as he drunk, usually just propped up against the bar on his own.'

'I see. Its sounds as though our Mr Robinson was not well liked, which will probably make this investigation much harder.'

'You can say that again,' Turner replied. 'I know not many liked him but I don't know any who would go as far as to kill him.'

'Mr Turner do you know why he had come to Whitby in the first place, or where he had come from?'

'He was also a private person, never told me anything about his life before coming here other than when he arrived in town. Although I always suspected he was looking for somebody, you know like a relative he was trying to find.'

'What makes you think this?' Matthews continued scribbling on his pad.

'He never made it that obvious but when we first met he asked me if I knew somebody, I can't remember the name now but the way he asked was as though it should be somebody around this area. He would always be scanning the street as though looking out for someone and I know he would ask around in the pubs, hence why he is known in them all.'

'And you can't remember what this name was…do you recall if the name was of a man or woman?'

'I couldn't be sure.'

'Mr Turner on the night that James was murdered, were you out drinking with him that night?'

'No, sir. He had asked me to join him for drinks at the Black Horse Inn, but I couldn't afford it. I usually joined him on a Friday after work when we got paid, nothing more.'

'Do you know if he made plans to go out with anybody else?'

'Not to my knowledge, but to be honest he went out for a drink most evenings so I presume he was alone but of course I couldn't be sure.'

'Can you tell me what time James left work that evening?'

'We usually knock off around six. I headed straight home. James was in a particularly cheery mood that day, but never said why. Begged me to go for a drink that evening, and got a little upset when I said no.'

'So once you clocked out of work that was the last you saw of him?'

'Yes detective, he headed over the bridge and towards Church Street. We spoke briefly walking towards the bridge but then I headed the opposite way to my house on Broomfield Terrace, its near Pannett Park.'

'Okay, well thank you for your time Mr Turner, if I could just get some details from yourself in case I need to speak with you again.' Mr Turner wrote down his name and address for the detective before returning to his work. Matthews followed him out of the office, and when back on the street thanked him again.

Harvey was still waiting outside the door and greeted the detective with a smile upon seeing him. 'Get anything, sir?'

'I think so, we finally have a name and address of where he was staying, so it's a start. Come on, let's get to the station, I should've been there hours ago.'

CHAPTER 8

By early afternoon, the Detective had managed to amass together two officers to question the residents of Havelock Place. Both given only the minimal information required of the case, as well as a pencil sketch of the victim that the chief had had arranged the previous day. Given the length of the street, Matthews knew they would be at it for the remainder of the day, if not longer; he knew from his days interviewing the public in York how much people loved to talk; especially when it involves a crime.

During this time, he had also been shown to his

new office by Mrs Lloyd-Hughes, his new secretary. She was in her late forties with dark hair that was cut into a bobbed style, and even in her small heals she didn't quite reach the detectives shoulder. She had large thick glasses which covered half of her face and yet she still seemed to squint as though she struggled to see. She wore a simple navy blue dress which had long sleeves and came up high on her chest.

Mrs Lloyd-Hughes was in fact the secretary to a number of senior members of the police station, but her desk was conveniently outside of Detective Matthews office in a small foyer. She greeted him as though they had known each other for years, and in some ways she had. She had worked in the offices at the station for a number of years and Matthews could remember her working on the front reception desk when he was a child.

'W-Welcome b-back.' She coughed into her handkerchief, and her voice was croaky as though she was unwell, and her words came out as though she was constantly out of breath. But Matthews knew that this was just her normal voice, although the coughing did seem to be much worse than he had remembered.

'Thank you Mrs Lloyd-Hughes, it is nice to see you again.'

'If you...' she started coughing again into her handkerchief, and once stopped took a long drag on her cigarette before continuing, 'if you need anything s-sir, just s-shout.' She coughed again, wheezing away as she returned to her desk chair, and Matthews headed inside the office.

He was grateful that his office was not too close to his fathers. It was a modest sized room with double windows that looked towards the police stables and training paddocks. He had a large solid oak desk, which he thought was completely empty, except one of the draws that was locked.

'Mrs...' He went to shout, but his secretary was already walking through his office door with a key in her hand, as though she had read his mind.

'F-Forgot to hand you this s-sir.' She spoke, trying her hardest not to cough again. 'The C-Chief handed it to me yesterday.'

She placed the key on the desk and let herself out again, wheezing as she went. Matthews immediately unlocked the draw to see inside a pistol with body harness, and laid on top was an official police badge. A brass, star shaped badge that was the size of Matthews palm. It had the crown of Queen Victoria on the top, and in the centre was a rose to symbolise the white rose of Yorkshire; and around the rose were the words "North Yorkshire Police". Matthews slipped the badge into his trouser pocket, but decided to leave the pistol there for now and relocked the draw.

He then decided to check out the rest of his modest office. There was a bookcase behind the door which was bare and covered in dust, and a dusty old fireplace in the corner that still had old burnt out coal in it from the previous occupant. The office had clearly lain vacant for some time and now inside and behind his desk the detective almost didn't know what to do with himself. He checked through his bag and decided to store certain items in his desk that he felt didn't need carrying around, he also checked through his notes to ensure he hadn't missed anything.

The stop off at the docks had really given him a boost of confidence having now finally gotten some information. He knew he still had a long way to go, but this small boost was making him feel much better about his new position. He lit a cigarette and rested his feet on the window sill besides him as he leaned back in his chair, after a minute or two he realised he had nowhere to put the ash from his cigarette and quickly walked over to the window, holding a hand underneath in case the ash was to drop prematurely. He flicked it outside. He could see Harvey in the courtyard brushing down the two horses whilst they stood and ate hay.

He then recalled his intention to visit the guest house James Robinson had been staying. Late afternoon was already fast approaching and so he grabbed his bag, placed his notebook back inside and headed out, cigarette still in one hand. On his way out he asked Mrs Lloyd-Hughes to make a note of any messages that came in, although he didn't expect any, she gave him a nod and smile as she continued typing on her typewriter.

'Where to now sir?' Harvey said upon seeing him

come into the courtyard. His face filled with joy at knowing Matthews had purposefully come to find him.

'To Church Street,' Matthews replied as he hopped inside the carriage whilst Harvey re-attached the horses, 'it's time to pay a visit to Mrs Sheppard's guest house.'

'Right-e-o.' Harvey slammed the carriage door shut and took his perch up front.

The ride to Church Street was short, and the hustle and bustle of the town soon surrounded them. The cobblestones of Church Street made for an uncomfortable ride, but thankfully it was not a very long street. They passed the White Horse and Griffin to the right, and then the market square to the left before coming to a stop outside a modest little building nestled between a newsagents and another guesthouse. It was three storeys tall, with a bright red door and window frames. The street was extremely narrow at this point and it was a struggle for Matthews to get out of the carriage as the building sat right against the constricted road side.

'Would you like me to wait for you sir?' Harvey asked from his perch up front. The carriage soon became surrounded by people all curious to why a police vehicle was there. A number of children surrounded the horses to pet them.

'I think it is probably better for you to move the horses back along the road where it was wider, you will probably struggle to turn around with these crowds anyway.' Harvey nodded and guided the horses forward away from the people in the hope to turn around. Matthews fought his way through the crowd of people to the front door of the guest house and banged on the door. Many of the onlookers waited to see what was going on, none of them disguising what they were doing.

'What's the matter constable, is she in trouble?' an elderly woman asked. 'I wouldn't be surprised, she's an odd ball if ever there was one.' The detective reframed from answering her question, and thankfully Mrs Sheppard finally opened the door. She didn't say anything at first and looked in shocked at the hoard of people surrounding her doorway. Beckoning the detective inside she seemed almost relieved to shut the door on the noisy crowd.

'I'm sorry, I couldn't hear myself think. Are you here to see me officer?' Mrs Sheppard's voice was soft and the surprise on her doorstep seemed to have thrown her off balance. She was barely concentrating on the detective and was still looking at the now closed door. She had dark grey hair that was short and curled, she wore no make-up and was dressed in a simple black dress that was dirty at the bottom where it grazed the floor. She had an apron on that was pale and patterned with flowers.

'Mrs Sheppard is it?'

'Huh? Oh…yes, that's me. Can I help you?' She finally took her eyes from the door and took the gaze of the man in front of her.

'Mrs Sheppard my name is Detective Matthews, I work at the Whitby Police Station…' he still wasn't used to his new title, and he almost slipped again by nearly saying York station, 'I am here because I believe a man named James Robinson has been staying at this guest house for some time, would that be correct?'

'That is correct detective, Room Three, he's been here since September.'

'Do you know of his whereabouts now?'

'I don't really pry into my guests' personal lives detective, I am quite happy to just let them be. He didn't join me for breakfast this morning, but then sometimes he doesn't come back if he got drunk or gone off with a girl. Mind, I've never had nobody stay here as long as him before though.'

'Do you find that strange Mrs Sheppard?'

'Well normal folk do just stay a couple of days, maybe a couple of weeks even, but rarely more than that. He's practically living here...but I don't mind, he pays his way like any other guest.'

'Mrs Sheppard the reason for my call is that yesterday morning a man was found on the beach, dead. We have reason to believe it was Mr Robinson.' A gasp was all she could manage, and she covered her mouth with one hand. 'Do you know if he had any relatives we could contact?'

'As I say son, I don't delve too much into guests'

personal lives. We barely ever had a real conversation. I know he worked at the docks, don't ask me which yard as I don't even know that.'

'Would you be willing to identify the body Mrs Sheppard, with no family I'm afraid we have nobody else.'

'I guess I could detective, if you're sure there is nobody else.'

'I was also wondering if I could take a look at his room, see if there is anything in there that could give us some more details on him or his family, or even anything that could indicate what happened yesterday.'

'Yes of course son, let me get you my spare key. I have one for all the rooms so I can give them a clean.' She shuffled off along the corridor, leaving Matthews by the front door. She wasn't gone long, and returned with a large metal key in her hand. 'Room Three, top of the stairs and to your right. If you need anything detective just shout.' With that she disappeared into the back, leaving the detective alone.

The stairs were narrow and creaked with every footstep he took. The smell of cigarette smoke filled the whole building and the walls leading upstairs were covered in damp and mould. Matthews found the room easily enough and before trying the key gave a gentle knock, just in case. There was no answer.

The door to the room was unlocked with a loud clunk, and the bottom of the door rubbed along the worn carpet making it an effort to open. The room itself was small, with a single bed. which had clearly been made up neat by Mrs Sheppard, and a small wooden bedside table with a half burnt candle rested upon it. There was a slender free-standing wardrobe at the base of the bed, and a thin dirty window that looked towards the harbour. To look at it the room seemed immaculate, but the detective soon came to realise that this was just a facade. Under the bed was rammed with what could only be described as junk, the two-drawer bedside table too was overflowing with mess inside, as was the wardrobe. He soon realised he was going to be here a while.

The underside of the bed was mostly littered with dirty clothing, with the occasional old payslip, and tissue and food wrappings that had clearly not made it to the dustbin. Matthews made sure to pull everything out just in case there was anything hidden at the back. The bedside draws were filled with clothing, mostly socks and underwear; there was also a fold out map of Whitby, as well as receipts for clothing and food shops, nothing from this pile stood out as being peculiar.

He drew his attention to the wardrobe. The clothing hung inside all looked the same, and piles of unwashed items were thrown in the bottom. Matthews checked there was nothing underneath them and even checked the pockets of each item. He turned his attention to inspecting the one and only shelve at the top of the wardrobe. There were only a handful of items here, a small shoe box and a Kelly & Co. Ltd 1881 addition of the *Whitby Directory*. He opened the shoe box and discovered it contained letters, hundreds of them, and not all from the same person. Scanning a handful he managed to identify that many of them were from the same person, yet there were certainly one or two other sets of handwriting that he could make out too. He would take the box with him and check through it more closely at his leisure.

Before leaving he decided to make sure anything he had touched was returned to its original place. He double checked there was nothing else up on the shelf out of view. There was only the directory book, which he lifted down and quickly thumbed through, not expecting anything out of the ordinary. To the detectives shock the interior of the book was covered in writing, crossings out and scribbles. Not all pages were defaced, and the detective flicked through a number of pages to see if there was any obvious pattern, but without looking through it more carefully it was difficult to tell. There was something about this James Robinson that didn't quite seem right, thought Matthew's, what exactly was he trying to achieve here?

CHAPTER 9

The detective left Mrs Sheppard's guest house, dismissed Harvey for the rest of the day and returned home by foot. It was now early evening on Friday and most of the shops in Whitby would soon be closed for the night. He stopped off at various places along the way for extra supplies. He still needed some better cleaning equipment for his house, as the sweeping brush he currently had looked as though his grandmother had had it since the beginning of time; and he had very little food in the house. With the small shoe box of letters tucked under his arm, and the *Whitby Directory* safely stored in his briefcase he took off along Church Street in the hope to catch a number of shops before they closed for the day.

With his father being the chief of police, and his mother having been a social butterfly around town Matthews couldn't go anywhere in Whitby without people knowing who he was. Most just said hello in passing, some were more intrusive and insisted on consoling him on his mother's recent death. Luckily for Matthews he was not one to feel pressured into hanging around for a conversation with anybody, especially when he had things to do.

Matthews managed to get to the general store for some more cleaning supplies, the bakery for what little supplies of bread they still had, and the fish mongers to make something for his dinner. Everyone that served him wanted to chat with him about his mother and father and welcomed him back to town. By the time he came to the door of the final shop, he nearly walked past it out of sheer exhaustion of hearing the same old questions. He was stood outside the greengrocers and decided he better go inside, otherwise he would be eating the fish he purchased on its own.

'Are my eyes deceiving me or has Benjamin

Matthews just walked through the door.' A young bearded man hollered with a deep husky voice. Matthews sighed at yet another interaction before realising who it was.

'It can't be little John Travers Cornwell, the scrawny kid who followed me around at school every day. What on earth are you doing in here…and behind the counter, not steeling things are you.' He joked, and the two men laughed. 'I thought you had joined the navy? Last I heard you'd gone to Plymouth, and had no intention of returning.'

Matthews dumped his bags in the corner and went to shake his old friends hand. John was twenty-four years old, the same as Matthews, yet his thick unruly beard, wiry hair and tired face made him look twice the age of the detective. He was tall like Matthews, and had bright blue eyes that stood out against his dark beard and pale skin, he had broad shoulders and was much more muscular than Matthews remembered. He was the typical tall, dark and handsome type.

'It sure is. Friends call me Jack these days.' The

two friends shook hands across the counter. 'Returned to Whitby only last week to be precise, this is my father's store. It's the best I have now that the navy discharged me.'

'Oh, why so?'

'Injury, I've been in hospital the last couple of months. An explosion shattered my leg, took them a long time to retrieve the shards of metal and glass lodged in there. Thought I might lose my leg at one point, but thankfully I still have it, be that with horrendous scars and I can't walk too far anymore…but it could have been much worse.'

'Jack I'm so sorry, I remember it was always your dream, it's all you'd talk about as a child.'

'Well I lived that dream, now it's time to find out what the next one is. I'll be dammed if I'm staying in this poky shop the rest of my life. By the way, I heard about your mother, my condolences to you and your family.'

'Thank you. We should go for a drink sometime, catch up properly.'

'I, that we should. Although I hear you are a big deal police officer now, is it okay for you to be seen out with a simple shop assistant like me.' Jack laughed, as did Matthews.

'I think I can make an exception for an ex-navy hero,' replied Matthews. The two men talked and talked until Jack realised that it was closing time. He served his friend for the items he wanted, some potatoes and carrots, and Matthews left him to close up.

The walk home was not long, but with armfuls of shopping the journey appeared longer than normal, he regretted sending Harvey and the carriage home. As he reached his house, he was surprised to see his sister Charlotte standing on the doorstep. She was a lot shorter than her brother, but had the same brown hair which she always tied up, and the same striking green eyes. She lived with their father, and was a school teacher in the town. Having only just turned eighteen she looked barely a child herself. Their mother's death had hit Charlotte the hardest, they were the closest in the family and spent so much time together that Charlotte was struggling to adjust. Matthews knew that his father had put in the request for Matthews return to Whitby in the hope it would make Charlotte happier, and for her to have somebody to fuss over no doubt.

'Ah… here you are,' she rushed to help him with his groceries, 'I wondered if you would be home.'

'Lotty, it is good to see you.' Matthews gave her a hug the best he could through all the items in his arms. 'What are you doing here?' He led her inside and she closed the door behind them.

'I knew you would be busy, father told me he has assigned you a case already; I told him that was a little unfair not to give you a day or two to settle in.' She looked around the kitchen as Matthews placed his shopping on the table. 'It certainly needs a bit of love in here doesn't it?'

'More than a bit I would say.'

'I brought you a couple of bits down, I didn't think you would have had time to shop, but I see I am too late.' She placed a basket besides his shopping. 'Just a small number of things I baked earlier today, there is always far too much for just me and father.' Matthews thanked her as he started to unpack his shopping. The cleaning items he left out, ready to tackle the house again. Charlotte offered to help, and assisted whilst her brother began cleaning the kitchen counters.

'It is good to have you back in Whitby, I never liked you being so far away.'

'I was only in York, Lotty, it was not exactly that far away.'

'I know, but we used to have tea together most nights, and that all stopped after you moved away. Mother was upset too, but she would never say because she knew it was what you wanted.' She spoke whilst standing on a stool wiping down the dirty window. Her brother besides her, cleaning out the bare cupboards that were filled with dust and cobwebs that must have been there for months.

'You know I didn't go to York to get away from you Lotty, but I wanted to be an officer and I couldn't do that on my own merit here with father as chief.'

'But surely you are pleased to be back, this house

is much bigger than the room you were renting in York, and being a detective is a promotion most officers only dream of.'

'It is not a promotion when it is handed to you for no other reason than your father being the chief. Lotty I would take that room in York any day over this filthy house and job. Father had no right in meddling in my career.'

'He was only trying to do right by you, he wanted you to have a secure job, a roof over your head; can't you at least be grateful for that.' She stepped off of the stool and threw the rag into the sink. 'You only have one family Benjamin, don't let your pride stand in the way of seeing a good opportunity.' She stormed out of the kitchen and headed for the front door, Matthews followed her.

'Don't leave Lotty, I don't wish us to argue.'

'I have to go, father will be wanting his dinner on the table when he gets home. I'll come back tomorrow if you like, you'll need help cleaning this place up, and I don't see you getting many offers to help. Let's be honest, I've only seen down here and it's going to take days just to get it respectable; I may need to come a couple of days as you can't do this and solve a case on your own.' She flung open the door and before he could answer she left, leaving Matthews in the doorway watching her march along the street. He knew his sister wouldn't stay mad at him for long, in fact her offer to come back and help showed she wasn't really that angry with him; but although Matthews could see his father's gestures were meant in a good way, he still saw them as an unearned achievement that the rest of the Whitby Police Force will see as a hand-me-down.

As he went to close his front door a distant voice caught his attention.

'Detective Matthews!' The voice shrieked up the street. He returned to the doorstep to see Harvey running along the road towards his house at full speed.

'What's the matter boy?' Harvey skidded to a halt, and through desperate breaths tried to speak.

'De-tect-ive...' he gasped. 'Come quick...the library closes in thirty minutes.'

'What are you going on about, come in and I will pour you a drink.'

'N… No t… time Detective. You need to c-come to the library with me now. I have found something that m-may tell us what the structure holding down the dead man was.'

'But surely it was simply something to restrain his body?'

'No detective, I think it is more than that.'

CHAPTER 10

Matthews raced inside for his hat and coat and was back at Harvey's side within seconds. The two of them barely spoke as they raced down the street and back towards the town.

'Why did you not bring the book to me?'

'I'm sorry, Sir,' Harvey spluttered, 'I do not have a library card and the librarian wouldn't let me take it.'

Matthews led the way down a narrow passage between two buildings as a short cut down to the harbour side where the library was located. Whitby had many of these dark narrow passages and Matthews knew them all like the palm of his hand. He had often heard Whitby being described as an ant's nest, with so many paths and passages leading off in different directions any unfamiliar traveller would easily become lost if strayed from the main streets.

As they approached the end of the alley, the sound and smells of the harbour started to become clear, and upon turning the corner Matthews slammed straight into an oncoming lady, nearly knocking both of them over.

'I do apologies Miss...' Matthews stopped, his hand still holding onto the woman's arm as he had tried to catch her from falling, and realised who it was. 'Grace, I do beg your pardon.' She retrieved her arm from his grasp, brushed down her dress as though wiping away any dirt, and recomposed herself.

'Well no harm done,' she said with a smile, 'good day detective.'

Grace was beautiful and elegant and charming,

but here before him now she stood with a cut under her eye and what was clearly the start of a bruise around it. 'Is everything okay?'

'Why would it not be, I am just returning home.' She continued passed him, but he quickly jumped back in front of her.

'Tell me, I know you wish to protect him, but did he do this to you?' She did not say a word and brushed passed him again.

'Detective,' Harvey called, Matthews ignored him and again blocked Grace's path.

'Grace please, I do not wish for you to get hurt. I need to know if he did this to you. Violence will not be tolerated and I can stop him, but you need to tell me.'

'Detective,' Harvey shouted again.

'Thank you for your concern detective, it is good to know that the police force has men who care for the citizens, but please do concern yourself with somebody who actually needs your help.' She again tried to pass him, but this time he took hold of her hand.

'Grace, don't let him win. Don't let him keep hurting you.'

'I would appreciate it detective if you unhanded me,' her voice turned angry, 'I do not wish for you to start idle gossip about me being beaten, this cut on my face was a simple accident in which I would like you to mind your own business. Now good day, detective.' She snatched her hands from his grip and took off along the pavement at a brisk walk, holding up her long dress slightly so she did not trip on it.

'Detective, please.' Harvey called.

The detective stood and watched Grace disappear around the corner. He then turned back to Harvey and they continued at speed towards the library.

'Harvey I would like you to do something for me.' Matthews sounded serious as he continued marching along the road.

'Yes detective?'

'I believe that Grace is in danger, and that she is

protecting her fiancé who is hurting her. I need you to keep an eye on her for me.' Harvey nodded and neither of them said any more on the subject as they reached the library.

When Matthews and Harvey entered the library, Harvey rushed off to retrieve the book and Matthews went to speak with the librarian who was sitting behind a tall counter.

'Good evening Ms, my name is Detective Matthews, I work at the Whitby police department…'

'I know who you are, you're little Benjamin Matthews, your grandmother and I were close friends.' The elderly woman smiled at Matthews. 'How can I help you?'

'I am working on a case and my…' for a moment he wasn't sure how to introduce Harvey, was he his assistant, his driver….what? '…my assistant wishes me to see something he found in a book that may help the case, do you mind if we take a quick look before you lock up.'

'Of course not detective, in fact it takes me a

while once I've locked the doors anyway, so take your time and let me know when you want to leave.' She took out her keys and started heading towards the doors, Matthews made his way through the aisles of tall bookshelves to find Harvey.

'I'm over here detective.' Came Harvey's voice, he had found a small seating area and was flicking through an old tatty book. 'Here detective, this is the page.' He handed over the book. There on the paper was a hand drawn sketch of the small fence like structure which had bound the victim.

'How did you come across this Harvey?'

'I'm sorry detective, I did something I know I'm not supposed to, but you see there is this girl who works at the library, she has gone home now, and I was telling her I was assisting you. Well I may have gone too far and told her a few things I shouldn't and I mentioned about the fence like restraint on the man. She told me about this ritual and told me that it would likely be written about in one of these books, and after a short search, I found it.'

'Harvey your wandering mouth is not

appreciated, especially in the means of impressing girls. However you do seem to have come across something, let's see what we have here.' He moved closer to a burning candle perched on a table, the library was quite dark back here away from the windows. Keeping hold of the page he needed, he turned the book over to inspect the cover. A simple old leather-bound book with a marble styled pattern on the front and back. The spine again covered in the brown leather, with a small square darker section with gold writing that read "History of Whitby". The book was certainly worn and smelt of old leather and paper combined. Matthews sneaked a look onto the first page to see if there was any more information on the book. On the inside cover was a fold out map of the town, and on the first page read the words "A History of Whitby and of Whitby Abbey". The authors name was Lionel Charlton and it read that this was one of three books regarding the history of the town. He turned back to the page Harvey had given him and began to read.

"Every year on the eve of Ascension Day the ceremony of the Horngarth, or the Planting of the Penny Hedge, takes place in Whitby's upper harbour. Ascension Day being chosen for the ceremony because it falls forty days after Easter Day, ensures that the tide is always low at the appointed time."

'So is it a religious ceremony?' asked Harvey.

'I'm not sure yet, did you not read this already?'

'Not really, I saw the picture of it and came straight to see you.' Matthews gave a snigger, amused by Harvey's eagerness and also his lack of checking facts. He turned back to the book and continued to read it out loud.

"The penny hedge is constructed with nine upright hazel stakes driven into the mud with an ancient mallet, nine 'yethers' or pliant branches for intertwining, and is braced at each end with 'strout-stowers'…It must be strong enough to withstand three tides."

'Well it certainly managed that.' Matthews smirked.

'But what is the point of it?' Harvey quizzed. Matthews scanned the page as though trying to find the part he wanted.

"In the fifth year of the reign of King Henry II, (1159) the Abbot of Whitby imposed a penance on three hunters, and their descendants for all time, for murdering a hermit at Eskdale. The hermit, who survived his injuries for three days sought to forgive the hunters and wished them no harm on the promise that they and their dependents enact a penance."

'What does that mean?' Asked Harvey.

'It means that he wished for them to perform a task. It looks like they were to make the penny hedge each and every year, on Ascension Day, and their descendants had to continue the penance every year.' Matthews continued scanning the story.

'When is Ascension Day?'

'It says forty days after Easter,' Matthews face screwed up for a moment whilst he tried to remember when Easter had been. 'I think Easter Sunday was the 29th March, or somewhere around the, which means that forty days later would be about the time it was made, but what I don't understand is why there was a body entangled in it this year. Nothing in this story mentions a sacrifice of any kind; the penny hedge is simply to be made to withstand three tides, that is all. So where did a body come from?'

'You also read that the penny hedge is built on the upper harbour, but this was on the beach. So maybe it's not the same.' Harvey said.

'Looking at the description, and the pencil sketch, I think it is certainly an exact match. The problem is why was is done on the beach, and what does James Robinson have to do with it all?'

'Does it say anything else?' Harvey enquired.

'It does say that the penny hedge ceremony must be performed under the supervision of the Bailiff of the Manor of Fyling. But considering I have never heard of the Manor of Fyling we may need to do a little more digging.'

CHAPTER 11

I t was Saturday morning and Detective Matthews had made a start cleaning his living room before his sister arrived. He knew she would arrive early, and as expected she knocked on the door at half past eight.

'Good morning,' she said in her naturally cheerful manner. 'I have brought with me some bi-carbonate of soda and some extra cloths and brushes for scrubbing the bathroom. Are you going out today working on the case?'

'I have a few things I want to do here first, like go through some old letters and what not, but yes I may pop out later.'

'That's not a problem, I figured you probably would be. Hence my helping or you would never get this place respectable.' She smirked and took her bags through to the kitchen. 'I'll put the kettle on the hob, a cup of tea will certainly start the day off on the right foot.'

Matthews returned to the living room and began cleaning the fireplace. It was grubby to say the least. Some of the ash and soot surrounding the open fire looked as though it had been there for decades. He knew he really needed to replace most of the furniture too, it was either broken or covered in layers of soot and dust; and he had still not had chance to change his uncomfortable bed.

'Still smells the same, doesn't it?' Charlotte returned with a tray of cups and biscuits, not the fanciest of display but it was clean, and in this house that was a blessing.

'It certainly does. I keep expecting her to walk around the corner any minute asking me what I'm doing here.' He took the tray off of his sister and placed it on the window ledge, fearing the coffee table may not be able to take the weight due to its mould ridden legs. His grandmother had collected furniture, as well as cupboards worth of items, throughout her life and had never liked to throw anything away. Their mother had done a good job at clearing the house after she had died, but there was still a long way to go.

'She would find it quite funny you living here.' Charlotte smirked. 'She loved this house, she'd be thrilled you are in it.'

'She may be less thrilled if she knew I wanted to replace most, if not all of the furniture. It's all long past its best.'

'My neighbour is selling some of his furniture as he's moving into a smaller house, I'll see what he has left for you.' Charlotte slurped her tea whilst perching on the window sill next to the tray. It was a little wobbly, but it was slightly cleaner than the seats. 'It may not be new things but he has good quality things, I'll pop in to see him later on my way home.'

'Thanks Lotty, I think I am going to need everything.'

They drank their tea and ate biscuits whilst reminiscing about their grandmother. Certainly, the matriarch of the family they had many a fun tale to re-call, and found themselves laughing and joking about all their old memories of her. When they finished their pot of tea Charlotte cleaned the cups whilst Matthews continued scrubbing the fireplace. She joined him back in the living room and began beating the cushions on the sofa out of the window, causing an almighty cloud of dust outside. There was a lull in conversation for a moment, as though neither one knew quite what to say to the other. They had always gotten on as siblings, but they had never really spent that much time alone in the last five or six years and had somehow become a little less connected.

'How is Pops coping without mother?' Matthews asked.

'It was hard at first, you know, the shock of it all I suppose,' Charlotte stopped beating the cushions for a second and sighed, 'it sort of feels like she has just gone away really, you know like when she used to visit her sister in Edinburgh. It's only been about a month since the funeral, yet these weeks feel like months.'

'And how are *you* coping?' Matthews hesitantly asked. 'It can't be easy on you living with *and* looking after father as well as working at the school.'

'Oh you know what he's like, so wrapped up in his work he is barely home or if he is he usually brings paperwork home to do. So, it feels more like living alone really. I see him for dinner, sometimes breakfast, and that is it really.'

'Has he not got you matched up with a suitor yet, it's all he used to talk about, getting you married into a good family.' Matthews smirked, he knew this irritated his sister and he had always teased her about it growing up.

'As a matter of fact, I've met a gentleman myself; father and mother both met him before she died.' She smirked back it him, looking proud of herself.

'Really?' he could not hide his surprise, especially given this was the first he knew about it, 'and who is this gentleman, do I get to meet him?'

'He's called John Nicholson,' she said with apprehension. Matthews looked at his sister confused, he recognised the name instantly, but surely she was winding him up?

'John Nicholson?' His expression of confusion changed to humour. 'Isn't he the owner of the local football club, he must be twice your age and surely still with his wife?'

'That's John Nicholson senior, I mean his son. He turned nineteen just a couple of months ago.'

'Oh thank goodness,' Matthews chuckled, 'and what does he do?'

'He plays for the football team but is also an apprentice at the steel yard where the ships are made. His father owns that too, but is starting him at the bottom with the plan on working him up to take over the company. He is in Sheffield at the moment, been there a week, they have quite a steel industry down there, but he is due back tonight.'

'Well, it seems you have it all planned out.'

Matthews sighed. 'That will be both my younger siblings married before me, what a disappointment I am,' he said it in a sarcastic tone.

'Oh certainly,' his sister teased, 'I couldn't possibly be seen with you out in daylight, an unmarried man at your age. People will wonder what is wrong with you.' She laughed and gave him a playful tap on the arm. 'You will find somebody brother,' her tone changed to be more serious, 'she is out there. But not if we don't get this house cleaned, goodness you would scare even the homeless dogs away with a house this filthy. Now then, I will head on upstairs, I won't get anything done with you talking to me constantly,' she again smirked, 'if you need to go out and do any detective work I don't mind.' With that she took herself off upstairs, where her humming could be heard as she cleaned.

Matthews finished cleaning his living room as best he could, and after a couple of solid hours it was looking much better, other than getting new furniture there was little more he could do. The kitchen he had managed to clean too, and with a quick tidy up of the downstairs landing he was done, or at least for today. Charlotte was still upstairs singing to herself and apart from taking her a drink, he left her to it. He wanted to make a start going through the box of letters he had found in the wardrobe of James Robinson.

The shoe box was filled with handfuls of letters, not all from the same person. The first one he came to read:

My Dearest James,

Your being away this long breaks my heart greatly. I think of you each day and wonder when you will return to me. You know I have always loved you more than anybody else in this world and would not wish to spend my life with anybody other than you. Promise me you will return soon.

L x

There were many letters from L, all of a similar nature, but none of them were signed with a full name, nor was there any indication where the letter had been sent from. It was not difficult to realise that they were from a lover, maybe even a wife, which made Matthews wonder why Mr Robinson had left his apparent life to come to Whitby.

Another pile of letters from a different sender soon caught the attention of the detective, the letters again had no clear indication of where they had come from, but the content did seem a little strange, and each of these letters was dated, which helped the detective to place them in order. The handwriting was messy, but still readable and the tone of these letters were much harsher than that of the loving one. Matthews managed to find what seemed to be the most recently sent, it was dated less than a week before Mr Robinson was found dead on the beach.

It read:

May 2, 1891

James,

I employ you to see reason. You are chasing a rumour that may not even be true. I told you everything I know before you left and here you are still in Whitby over eight months later with no more information than I gave. Stop this foolish witch hunt now and return home, before you get yourself into anymore trouble.

WB

There was a lot of letters from WB, each one cryptic and telling James Robinson to stop what he was planning and return home. Just like the other letters, WB never wrote his full name, neither did he put anything in the letters as to what he was advising James against.

Matthews turned his attention to the Kelly & Co. Ltd 1881 addition of the *Whitby Directory*, which he had also taken from the victims' wardrobe. The directory was filled with crossings out, random scribbles and torn out pages, it would take a lifetime to work through it to see if anything was actually useful. He flicked through almost the entire book without anything standing out. Names were crossed out on random pages, others were circled and some pages had been torn out completely. He was certainly going to need much longer to sit and crack any potential pattern.

Matthews knew what he really needed to do was visit some of the bars that James Robinson spent his evenings, he hoped that speaking to some of the regulars might lead him to something useful he could work with. As today was Saturday he knew tonight would be an ideal time, as most bars were at their busiest. He knew that Robinson had been barred from a number of the public houses in town, but recalled his work colleague mentioning his intention to visit The Black Horse Inn the evening of his death.

It was now mid-afternoon and a knock on the door startled him. He wasn't expecting anybody but half anticipated it to be his father to see how things were going. It was not his father, but a young junior officer.

'Detective Matthews?' his deep voice whispered. He was a tall muscular man who was barely out of his teenage years, and looked a little nervous.

'Yes,' Matthews replied.

'Detective I have been sent to give you this letter, and also bring you news.' He handed the letter over and Matthews waited for the news.

'Well, go on.'

'Sir, I have been on Havelock Place again today with another officer finishing questioning the residents regarding the murder. Most residents had heard about it but none knew of the man.'

'I see, well we tried, good day.' He went to close the door on the young officer.

'Wait,' he said, the most animated he had been the entire time, 'there is more.' Matthews sighed, and returned the door to its open state.

'Be quick man, I am busy.'

'One of the residents sir, didn't know anything about the victim, but has admitted to building the wooden fence like contraption that held the victim. She called it a penny...erm, something.' The young officer rubbed his forehead as he tried to recall what he had been told. Matthews froze for a moment.

'What house number?'

'Number five, Sir.'

'Thank you officer.'

Matthews slammed the door, and headed for the

kitchen to retrieve his hat and coat. The letter in his hand almost forgotten for a moment. He quickly ripped it open at the kitchen table, it was from Mr Waters, the coroner.

Detective,

I have now completed my initial examination of the body. I can determine that the man's cause of death is drowning. He was not dead before coming to the beach. However, given the strange circumstances surrounding how he was discovered I intend on doing further examinations, and should anything come to my attention I will inform you.

Mr K.Waters

Matthews read the letter over twice. Not dead before? He was puzzled. How could a man like James Robinson, who looked as though he could take on most professional boxers, struggle in a little wooden contraption that could be snapped over by a child. It just didn't add up.

He folded up the letter and placed it in his brief case for later, shouted upstairs to his sister that he was going out, and raced outside. He couldn't believe he already had somebody admitting to have made the penny hedge, and he was certainly apprehensive to find out who this person was.

CHAPTER 12

Detective Matthews walked to Havelock Place, it was only two streets away from his own house on East Crescent. He had with him his briefcase, with notebook inside ready to interview the person who knew about the penny hedge. He was trying to imagine what kind of a person he would be speaking to, especially now knowing that James Robinson was not dead before being tied to it. As he walked, he couldn't help but think of his life back in York, and how he wished to still be there. He may have only been a constable in York, but it was more than he wanted. Here in Whitby as a detective he had never felt so far out of his comfort zone; the most difficult part of his job in York was chasing common thieves and trying not to fall over in the uneven cobbled lanes. He had helped on a number of bigger cases in York too, but had never been in charge of a case. He was used to getting statements from people, and even comforting those he had to deliver bad news too; but never had he been the sole, or lead investigator of a crime. His father's promoting him, not to mention transferring him back to Whitby, he had to admit was a lavish gesture that he could see was done in good faith. Many officers would certainly jump at the offer, but Matthews hated knowing that the promotion was due to his father's own wish and not his own personal achievement.

As he approached the house on Havelock Place his eyes wandered on towards the doorway of Mr O'Sullivan, the gentleman who found the body. Strange to think, he thought to himself, that the person who found the body is just two doors away from the person I am putting on the top of the suspect list. He hadn't even met the person at number five Havelock Place yet, but if they are admitting to making the penny hedge then he knew it was the closest to a suspect he had so far.

Matthews knocked on the large wooden, black painted door with a brass handle and knocker, and waited. The occupant appeared moments later, and the detective was slightly surprised by the person stood before him. It was not a muscular young man who could tackle Mr Robinson as he had expected, but instead he was greeted by an older woman clearly in her late sixties.

'Can I help you sir?' she spoke softly and smiled warmly at him. She looked tiny compared to the detective, and had snow white hair that sat on top of her head in tight curls. She had a pale complexion but wore makeup that made her cheeks slightly pink. She wore a long black dress that had delicate embroidery on from the waist up. She smelt extremely floral mixed with bi-carbonate of soda.

'Good afternoon madam, are you the occupant of this house?'

'I am sir. Are you the detective they told me was coming?'

'My name is Detective Matthews, I was

wondering if you could answer some questions, could I come in?'

The woman stood back and gestured for him to come inside. As soon as he stepped into the house the heat hit him. The detective was directed into the living room, and despite it being May, and being a lovely day outside, she had a grand fire burning in the fire place. Matthews could feel himself sweating before he had even taken a seat at a small table and two chairs by the window.

'Would you like a drink detective, I could do you a cup of tea, I've just made a pot.'

'Oh no thank you Mrs…I'm sorry I didn't catch your name.'

'Hutton, Ms Allison Hutton.'

She took the seat opposite him; the small wooden table was only just big enough for the bay window, and the two seats had cushions to sit on that were so worn they didn't give any padding what so ever. The living room was not overly large, but had in it a small sofa, and an arm chair that looked as though it was used more than anything else. It had a pile of knitting wool next to it, and a small table with a packet of tobacco and cigarette papers, as well as a bag of prescription tablets and an empty tea cup that had clearly just been finished. The walls were reasonably bare, with a small round mirror above the fire and a painting of Whitby abbey on the wall opposite.

'Ms Hutton my colleagues tell me that somebody at this address has confirmed they made a small wooden structure on the beach two days ago, I have reason to believe it may have been a penny hedge?'

'That is correct detective, I made it.' Her soft voice was so delicate and she seemed so rather concerned about the whole thing.

'Did my colleague tell you about the body that was found?'

'Yes sir, I was most shocked. He showed me the picture but I'm afraid I have never met the gentleman before, the officer who came couldn't remember his name and I'm afraid I do not know either.'

'Ms Hutton can I ask you when you made the

penny hedge?' Matthews took out his notepad.

'It was on Wednesday evening, I should have done it in the morning before the tide came in but I haven't been too well these past two weeks and I didn't make it in time, so had to do it later in the day.'

'Can I ask you why you made it?'

'Oh, it has been a tradition in my family for longer than I could say. You already knew it was a penny hedge so I will presume you know the story about the hermit that was murdered at the abbey in 1159. Well the planting of the penny hedge has been a tradition ever since. Some say it is a silly old tale that isn't true, but my family have all been involved in helping to make it. Sadly, I am the last one left, I have no children myself and fear the tradition will end with me.' She let out a small chesty cough and retrieved a handkerchief she had stored up her sleeve.

'From the information I read about the ceremony the hedge is usually constructed not on the beach but further up the harbour, so why did you do it so close to the town this time?'

'As I mentioned detective, I have been unwell these last two weeks, I did set off with the intention to do it in the normal spot but I was out of breath by the end of the street, so decided not to travel far. I have barely left the house these past two weeks, the doctor has been three times but tells me it is a simple chest infection that will pass.'

'Can I ask you…' he was interrupted by the living room door creaking open. A young man, who looked to be in his late teens, walked in. He had messy brown hair and wore beige trousers and a grey cotton shirt. He looked most put out to see the detective, as though he had ruined what he was planning to say to Ms Hutton.

'Oh sorry, I didn't know you had company.' His voice was low and slow like one would expect a sloth animal to speak, his voice and general appearance was sleepy.

'No need to apologies Willy, this is Detective Matthews.' Ms Hutton introduced him, Matthews stood and held out a hand to shake the young man's hand, but he winched backwards as though shocked and confused by this gesture and looked past the detective as though he was not there.

'I'll leave you alone then,' he spoke in his sleepy tone. 'I'll be in the kitchen.' With that he left the room in a hurry.

'Ms Hutton does that young man live here?'

'No, well yes I suppose he probably does now. He wasn't supposed to be staying but never really left. You see he is my nephew. My sister is no longer with us, God rest her soul, and her daughter lives in London now. Willy here came to stay with me when she passed last year, he's a good boy but couldn't handle living in a city like that.' She paused, looked at the doorway listening to check he had indeed gone before turning back to the detective and whispering, 'He's twenty-three, but doctors says he has the mental age of a twelve-year-old. I don't fully understand what he has, they gave it some long name, but he struggles with new situations or new people. He is a good boy, and helps me around the house. I can't really give him anything too complex to do, but he is good company. He never leaves the house though, mostly fear and panic with new people and situations, and so I give him little jobs to keep him occupied.' She sighed, still staring at the door.

'Ms Hutton when the officer came before with the picture of the victim was Willy here at the time, did he get to see the picture too?'

'Yes detective, we both spoke to the officer together, neither of us recognised him.'

'Ms Hutton, the information I read about the penny hedge said that it had to withstand three tides, does it then surprise you that it was still almost in tack the next morning.'

'I must admit detective I was a little surprised to hear that, normally it gets washed out to sea. It has been quite a calm week though, the weather has been settled which is not usual for Whitby, so this will make for a calmer sea. I suppose where I put it on the beach might have not been as deep as the harbour gets, it was just by the beach huts as I didn't have the energy to walk to the sea edge that was completely out, but still it astonishes me to hear it was still standing.'

Detective Matthews could feel the sweat pouring down his face and back. The blazing fire crackled away and yet Ms Hutton looked as though she was perfectly comfortable with the heat.

'Before I go Ms Hutton, the text I read also mentioned that the penny hedge ceremony must be witnessed by the Bailiff of the Manor of Fyling?'

'Oh yes,' she chuckled, 'well that text you read is probably describing the original ceremony. Fyling Manor is no longer there, in fact it was turned into a school at one time, but sadly it is no longer standing, I'm not sure when it was knocked down. I make the penny hedge alone these days, I find it a rather relaxing task.'

Desperate to leave, and starting with a headache due to the heat of the sitting room Matthews could no longer think of any more questions and decided it was time for him to vacate.

'Thank you for your time, Ms Hutton.' He stood to leave, and she followed him through to the front door. 'If you think of anything, or hear anything please do let me know. I may also need to come back too if anything else comes up.'

'Not a problem at all detective, I don't often go out and if I do it is not far.' She chuckled and gave him a little wave as he headed on back down the street.

It was already approaching evening, and Matthews still didn't feel any closer to having any strong leads on the case. He would return home to eat and freshen up. Tonight he would visit the Black Horse Inn public house, where he hoped to speak with some of the regulars who may have known Mr Robinson.

CHAPTER 13

The Black Horse Inn, was said to be the oldest public house in Whitby, and as Matthews arrived outside it he could certainly believe it from its tired exterior. Once called The White Horse, it had been renamed sixty years prior. The exterior of the building had been modernised when it had changed its name, however the interior was much, much older. Lit only by the single candles burning on the tables it was a dark dingy bar. Not a large place by any means, and had an over powering smell of ale, cigarette smoke and body odour. It was filled mostly with men, most of whom were playing cards, or talking and laughing loudly and generally out to get drunk.

'A pint please,' Matthews asked once he had made his way to the bar through the hordes of people. He was served by a young lady in the tightest corseted dress imaginable. She had red hair that fell in wavy curls around her shoulders and wore quite a lot of make up for someone, in Matthews opinion, so young. 'Is the landlord around tonight Miss?' She handed the detective his drink, took his money and then pointed at a man perched on a stool at the end of the bar. 'Thank you.' He said to the barmaid, but she had already gone.

Matthews made his way over to the landlord, he was a large man in his early fifties, he was clean shaven and had short brown hair that was receding at the front. His bellowing laugh echoed around the room as he spoke to an equally large man on the stool next to him. He held a silver cask ale pewter, which was clearly his own personal pint holder.

'Excuse me,' Matthews nudged his way to the man's side, 'are you the landlord?'

'Yes son,' the man replied with a gruff voice, not

even caring to look around at Matthews, 'but you best not be complaining about nuffin, I ain't your blinking babysitter.'

'Erm… no, sir. My name is Detective Matthews and I was wondering if I could have a quick word with you?'

The landlord turned to face Matthews, a serious expression crossed his face. He looked the detective up and down as though trying to sus out if he was genuine or not. Matthews took out his police badge from his trouser pocket and showed the landlord so as not to attract other attention. With a huff the landlord stood and beckoned the detective to follow him. They didn't go far, but to a doorway that had a sign above it reading "Staff Only".

'What's this all about then detective, another punch up in the street again? Look I try mi best to get rid of trouble makers but I can't stop em all. You know what drunk men are like that get a bit boisterous.'

'Mr… erm, I'm sorry I didn't get your name.'

'Henneberry. Michael Henneberry, landlord for

ten years. I don't need to ask your name, you're the chief's son ain't ya.' Matthews insides were screaming with anger, but he kept his composure and continued with his questions.

'Mr Henneberry, do you know who a Mr James Robinson is?'

'Name don't ring any bells son.' The detective pulled out the pencil sketch of the man he was referring to and showed the landlord. 'Ah, now that helps,' he said with slight apprehension, and he tapped his chin with his fingers as he tried to remember.

'Did you know this man Mr Henneberry?'

'No, not really. He came in here quite a bit, and come to think of it I even threw him out a couple of times too when he got rowdy but I never knew him to speak to. He was the one in the paper the other day weren't he.'

'Yes.' Matthews put the picture back in his case. 'Do you know anything at all about this man, or know of anybody that may know him a little better, does anybody in the bar now, for example, associate with him?'

Mr Henneberry turned his head back to the bar and scanned the room, he was a tall man and had to bend down just to fit into the door way.

'See that man over there with the blonde hair, wearing overalls. That is Timothy Oldman, he and your young gentleman were often squaring up to one and other, each one thinking they were better than the other. Pure male ego if you ask me, neither of em have a decent bone in their body. Anyway, the night your man died I threw the pair of them out of here. Fighting they were and I had had enough of it, told them that they either sorted it out or needn't return. Next day he's dead on the beach.'

'Thank you Mr Henneberry for your time, I will go and speak to him.'

'Hold your tail son, I ain't finished yet.'

'I'm sorry, do you know more?'

'You asked me if I knew people that knew your man, well Mr Oldman over there was somebody he fought with, but I think you may also want to speak with someone he was close to him on a more personal level.' The landlord gave Matthews a look that the detective took as being, somebody romantically involved.

'Do you know the name of this person?'

'Oh yes detective, in fact she has just this minute walked in. Miss Annie Rice.'

Detective Matthews swung his gaze back to the smoke-filled room and saw a young lady walking through the crowd, she was quite pretty and wore a low-cut dress which caught the attention of nearly every man in the room. Matthews could tell straight away that she was a prostitute but did not ask Mr Henneberry this out right. He simply thanked the landlord for his time and followed Miss Annie Rice as she headed back towards the door.

'Miss, oh Miss…could I have a word with you?' He caught her just before she headed back outside, she turned to look at him and smirked with delight.

'Hello sir, I seem to have caught your eye haven't I.' She said in a playful and most certainly flirtfull way, she then tapped his nose with her finger and winked.

'Miss Rice, is it?' She nodded, looking suspicious that he already knew her name. 'I was wondering if you knew a Mr James Robinson?'

'Who wants t'know?' Her tone changed and became more stand offish towards the detective.

'My name is Detective Matthews and I have been assigned to his case. I presume you are aware he is dead.' Her harsh expression softened, but she still looked at the detective with caution.

'I heard, yeah, shame…he was a good un.'

'Good in what way? I heard he didn't have many friends.'

'Let's jus say we kept each other company one or two nights a week, and he was certainly good at it.'

'Did Mr Robinson ever talk to you on a personal level, for example do you know anything about his personal life before he moved to Whitby?'

'Not much to tell ya the truth,' she started biting her nails, 'he has a wife back down south somewhere. Didn't usually have much good to say about her, cheated on him I know that. But don't know any more than that.'

'Did he ever tell you why he had come to Whitby?'

'Nah, as I say we rarely talked when we were together. Wanted me to satisfy his needs then usually left. Did tell him he could talk to me but said I had a big mouth.' She sniggered at her own comment.

'Is there anybody in town you think may wish to hurt Mr Robinson?' asked Matthews, becoming irritated with her as she began to ignore him and look over his shoulder to scan the room. 'Miss?' He tried to gain back her attention.

'What? Oh yes, hurt him. Well he certainly made plenty of fucking enemies in town, his biggest problem being his gambling addiction. That's the main reason he got barred from so many pubs, run up debts with so many people and can't afford to pay them back. He wasn't one to hide his opinions too, which also got him into trouble. Fights broke out most nights because of him, and I wouldn't be surprised if one of them beat him to death.'

'By "one of them" can you tell me any names?'

'Well I know they often hold gambling nights late at the Duke of York, usually hosted by Damian Campbell, known by his associates as DC. Bit of an arsehole if you ask me, and can't satisfy if he tried even if he does pay a lot.' She gave a quick eyebrow raise to emphasise her innuendo. 'He has James Robinson beaten on a regular basis by his gang for not paying off his gambling debts. He was barred from the Duke of York for the debts but they still hunt him out for the money, if he can't' pay they beat him. I found him laid in a ditch one night with blood all over his face after one of their beatings.'

'Can you think of anybody else who may want to hurt him?' Matthews asked, scribbling down notes as she spoke.

'Just one other name comes to mind. Johnny King. Although being on the force you will probably know his name already. James owes Johnny so much money for drugs it is unbelievable. Last I heard

Johnny had finally given James a deadline to pay otherwise he was going to break his legs. Fuck knows if it was him though who killed James. If it's right what they said in't paper then it don't sound like his style, if you know what I mean.' She lit up a cigarette and blew a large cloud of smoke into the detective's face. 'We done 'ere now then? I don't know any more and you're scaring away clients with your notepad.'

'One last question, do you know if Mr Robinson had any close friends in Whitby or relatives?'

'Nah, don't think so. Often saw him drinking with a guy who he worked with but that's it. I know he was sleeping with some slut over on the west coast too on a regular basis, Ellen Garner. Married woman but her husband is always away, always known for sleeping around that whore.' Matthews found her choice of words ironic considering her profession. 'Anyway, that's all I know so can I go now?'

'Just quickly Miss Rice, did you see Mr Robinson on Wednesday night. The landlord tells me he was thrown out for fighting?'

'Yeah, must have been around midnight. Got thrown out with another guy, but the other guy left straight away. James was completely pissed and could barely walk. I offered to take him home but he swore at me and told me to go away. He started headed the wrong way down Church Street, you know from where he was living. I tried to correct him and point him in the right direction but he just swore at me and said he wasn't going that way, so I let him head the opposite way. Although given how uneasy he was on his feet he wasn't getting anywhere in a hurry. I saw Damian Campbell's men approaching him so decided I didn't want to watch him getting beaten and went into the pub instead. When I came out nearly half an hour later none of them were around.'

'Thank you Miss Rice. If you think of anything else that could be useful, please do come and see me at the police...'

She didn't even let him finish as she ran out the door. Matthews finished scribbling down his notes, placed his pad back into his bag and returned to the bar, he finished the drink he had left on the bar and ordered himself a refill. When his second pint arrived he realised that the man who had just approached the bar to be served next to him was his friend, ex-navy officer John Travers Cornwell.

'Matthews,' he slapped his friend on the back, 'join me for a drink my friend.'

'Will do Jack, just give me a minute, I need to speak with somebody over in the corner.' He tapped his friend on the shoulder, pushed his pint closer to him to look after, and headed over to speak with Timothy Oldman.

'Excuse me sir,' he stood next to the man in overalls, his blonde hair stood out in the room against all the brown and black haired men. He was sat a table with four other men also in overalls, 'I was wondering if I could have a quick word?' Timothy Oldman looked at the detective as though he was scum, and waved his hand at him as though telling him to go away. 'Mr Oldman my name is Detective Matthews and I need to speak with you regarding an incident you were involved with on Wednesday night.' Timothy ignored the detective and pretended as though he had not heard him. 'Mr

Oldman if you refuse to co-operate then I will have no choice but to take you into the station under arrest so that you will have to answer questions there. I'm sure you would much prefer to have a quick word now to avoid that?' Oldman's face tensed with anger and he placed his pint glass onto the table and stood, turning his back to his friends he stood squarely up against the detective.

'What?' he said with an undertone of aggression.

'On Wednesday night, I have been informed that you were thrown out of this pub with a Mr James Robinson for fighting, is that correct?'

'Yes.'

'As it stands Mr Oldman you are thought to be one of the last people to see Mr Robinson alive that night. Could you tell me what happened after you were thrown out?'

'I ain't goin' to pretend I cared about the guy detective, he was a thug and a crook, and I for one am pleased he got what was coming to him. Cocky bastard had been asking for it for long enough. If you want to know why the fight happened it's because he thought he would start mouthing off about my wife, calling her all kinds of things. He's never met her and was just trying to piss me off, so I'll admit I threw the first punch.'

'Did you continue the fight out onto the street Mr Oldman?'

'No. He was so pissed out of his head I couldn't be arsed. He was rolling on the floor and couldn't even stand, I may have given him a kick but other than that I walked away.'

'Can I ask where you went?'

'I headed home, you can ask the wife, she'll tell you I was home.' His tone continued to vent anger, 'I don't know where that Robinson guy went to, but I can tell ya he weren't with me.' With that Timothy Oldman turned his back on the detective and re-joined his friends at the table. Matthews decided not to push his luck any further, especially since Mr Oldman had clearly had a number of drinks already this evening; Matthews could smell it all over his breath. He knew he needed to figure out what happened to James Robinson between leaving the bar and ending up dead on the beach; and he knew it was not going to be an easy task. He did however have some more names to now look into.

CHAPTER 14

It was Sunday morning, and Detective Matthews was getting himself ready for church. He had barely gone to church whilst living in York, and he hadn't really given it too much thought since returning to Whitby. That was until his sister had asked him to join the family whilst she was over cleaning the previous day. She had certainly done a marvellous job; the entire house now looked and smelt better than Matthews could ever remember it doing when his grandmother had lived there. She had even gone over the bits he had done, clearly deciding he had not done it nearly as well as she would have liked.

There was a church just around the corner from his house, but his family had always preferred to go to St Mary's Church on the east cliff, at the top of the one hundred and ninety-nine steps. It was his mother that had insisted on this, she found the setting on top of the cliff, overlooking the harbour below, and looking out onto the sea a much more pleasant location. His mother had been quite a free spirit during her life; preferring to spend time on the beach collecting shells, or in the woodlands picking wildflowers. She was always seen as an odd match to Matthews father, he couldn't have been any different if he had tried, yet their love for one and other was undeniable.

Matthews walked to the church alone. He was half asleep after spending the entire evening with his friend Jack at the Black Horse Inn. He had only gone to question a handful of people about his investigation but ended up returning home a little worse for where after midnight. He hadn't seen his friend Jack in so long, yet they spoke all night as though they had never been apart. After telling Jack about his police career in York and his return to Whitby, Matthews had been keen to hear all about

Jack's adventures as a navy officer. They spoke for hours, and time seemed to pass them both by unknowingly, which surprised them both when the landlord called for last orders.

When he reached the top of the one hundred and ninety nine steps his sister Charlotte was already there waiting for him. Matthews stopped on the final step to catch his breath; he had forgotten quite how steep they were. During his moments pause he glanced back down to the town below him, he had to agree with his mother, it was a stunning location for a church. The scene from the top was always changing with every season, and the buildings below appeared so diminutive and bunched together in the little town. The rows and rows of chimneys that lined the tightly packed streets were only broken up by the River Esk, which was lined with hundreds of fishing boats all the way down to the harbour entrance that led out to the open sea. The two large stone build piers that framed the end of the river harbour looked even more impressive from this angle.

The church itself was a charming stone building

that was surrounded by a graveyard that stretched from the cliff edge, all the way back towards the walls of the enormous abbey in the next field. St Mary's church looked tiny compared to the abbey, which dominated the landscape, and could be seen from almost everywhere in Whitby. The abbey had laid in ruins for hundreds of years, yet despite this it was the most iconic landmark in the town; a shell of its former glory, the abbey still managed to command all the attention away from the little church.

'Daddy has gone in ahead to get us seats,' Charlotte said whilst pulling him in for a hug, 'but first I want to introduce you to somebody.' Matthews hadn't noticed the young man watching them with anticipation. The church yard was filled with so many people talking and heading inside that the man had simply blended into the mass. 'This is John Nicholson.' Her voice had an air of nerves about her.

'Pleased to meet you.' Matthews extended a hand in greeting, realising at once that this was in fact the man she had told him she had been seeing. He was shorter than Matthews by nearly a foot, yet still taller than Charlotte. He had mousey brown short hair, and was trim built. He too looked a little nervous to be meeting Charlottes brother. Like most gentlemen he was wearing his Sunday best for church, a bowler hat cradled under his arm. 'You met the old man yet?' Matthews smirked.

'Yes, a couple of times now,' he spoke fast, 'pleasant man, gets on well with my own father.'

Matthews smiled and nodded, not really knowing what more to say to a man he had only just met. He was used to asking questions in his job, the questions were simply led by the events he was investigating, but social conversations with somebody he didn't know were often lost on him after the initial hellos. Once he knew somebody more, he could hold a conversation better, but with new people he always seemed to struggle. He found himself nodding and smiling awkwardly as he tried to think of something to break the moment's silence.

'We have something to tell you.' Charlotte took John's hand, an enormous grin surfaced on her face.

'John has asked me to marry him, he asked father's permission last night upon returning from Sheffield.' She gave out a small high-pitched squeal and took off her gloves to reveal a beautiful blue sapphire engagement ring. John smiled and looked anxiously at Matthews for some kind of a reaction.

'Oh…erm…yes, congratulations.' Matthews was a little taken a back, his sister hugged him again without warning and once released he again shook John's hand in congratulations, hoping his sister would simply leave it at that. He didn't disapprove, on the contrary, but reacting to sudden surprises that required some kind of reaction were never Matthews strongest abilities. He usually needed a pre-warning of something so he could see how he felt about it, rather than have it sprung on him and expected to give an instant reaction.

He followed his sister and her new fiancé into the church, his father had saved them all a pew near the back. Matthews exchanged pleasantries with his father, but little more. He was still angry with him and did not wish to pretend to play happy families with him just yet. Charlotte was determined to sit between John and her brother. Matthews took the aisle seat gladly and heard as Charlotte whispered to John, 'I told you he would like you.'

A moment later Matthews saw Grace, the young lady from the train, walk into the church, her arm intertwined with her fiancé. She didn't see Matthews as she walked past, but he noticed her. She was wearing a long blue dress with matching hat. All of the women in church were wearing hats today of a variety of colours, but Grace stood out to the detective as being the most beautiful. He could sense her awkwardness towards her fiancé, and the way in which he held her. A somewhat possessive grasp rather than a romantic lovers hold. She still had the black eye that Matthews knew had been given to her by him, even if she did deny it. He could see that she had tried to cover it up with make-up, but this seemed to only make it stand out more. She was clearly conscious of it too as she kept her head down as she made her way towards an empty seat.

As the final few people took their seats Matthews spotted Harvey lingering around the doorway. Upon catching the detectives eye he gave a crooked smile that said 'all is well' before retreating back outside.

The service began and Matthews found himself watching Grace the entire time. He barely heard the vicar's sermon at all, and the hymns he simply listened to…or at least listened to his sister screeching them in his ear. He didn't realise that somebody could sing a hymn so out of tune, but she certainly proved him wrong. She was tone deaf, but loved to sing her heart out as loudly as possible.

When the service was over Grace was ushered back up the aisle towards the door. Matthews quickly jumped into the aisle so as to catch her eye. She saw him, gave him a faint awkward smile that Matthews also read as 'please don't make a scene'. Her fiancé also caught sight of the detective and dragged Grace passed him with a scowl. Matthews wished beyond anything that he could help her escape that man, but with no proof, and her protecting him, there was nothing he could do.

Back outside and with the congregation making their way back down the one hundred and ninety-nine steps, Matthews and his family held back to let the mass disperse.

'We are having a big dinner this evening, of course you'll be coming?' Charlotte asked in a way that left Matthews unable to refuse, all the while clinging to John's arm. Surprisingly to Matthews, John too seemed keen, and agreeing with his wife-to-be he looked as Matthews as though his answer would confirm or deny his approval of him, he held onto Charlotte as though she were a trophy to be proud of. Matthews couldn't deny how happy they looked together; their father however stayed quiet, although Matthews was sure he heard him tut.

'Sure, what time?'

'Shall we say dinner at six, but you could come around sooner if you'd like to? We are all heading there now, and we have wine and cheese to have this afternoon whilst dinner is cooking.'

'Maybe, we'll see.'

Matthews gave his sister a kiss on the cheek, shook John's hand and gave his father an awkward smile before turning to leave. He wasn't aiming for the one hundred and ninety-nine steps, but instead was headed around the church to the graveyard. His family had already visited his mother's grave before the service, but he had decided to do it afterwards, alone.

The graveyard was still filled with clusters of people, churchgoers like himself who had come to pay their respect to deceased family and friends. Matthews hadn't visited his mother's grave since her funeral only the month before and wasn't sure exactly how he would feel.

'Detective...' came a voice from behind. He turned and was surprised to see Harvey again.

'Is everything alright?'

'Yes sir, I just wanted to tell you what I have seen following Grace...you know like you asked me.'

'Go on.'

'Yesterday I found her at the market, she was buying vegetables. I followed her home and not long afterwards I could hear shouting coming from inside. It didn't last long as a man left through the front door, swearing he was as he slammed the door behind him. I didn't see which way he went, but it must have been late before he came home as I didn't see him get back, and I was there till nearly ten.'

'Thank you Harvey, I appreciate you doing this. I just need her to see sense and speak up against him.'

Harvey bit the detective a good day and left. Matthews returned to search for his mother's grave.

It didn't take him long to find it, as the graveyard was not overly large. It perched on the cliffside with the town and sea below, and the cries of seagulls flying overhead. The grave of his mother was small and simple, with a fresh bunch of flowers which had clearly just been left by Charlotte. Being a new grave, it did not yet have a tombstone, and a simple wooden cross with his mother's name on was all that showed him he was at the correct spot.

He stared at the grave for what felt like the longest of times, and yet he felt nothing. This place did not make him feel anything but cold. His mother had been such a colourful person, with warmth and laughter filling her life, yet standing here now seeing her grave he wondered if she could see it too from where ever she was.

'You would probably find it funny seeing me standing her speechless,' he said in a whisper. 'You always knew exactly what to say, a trait I never seemed to get.' He regretted not bringing flowers now too. 'I met John, Charlotte seems happy with him. She told me you met him when they first started courting. It is nice seeing her smile again, I didn't think we would see that for a long time after we lost you...' His voice broke slightly, but he managed to reframe from crying.

He spent approximately ten minutes at his mother's grave, and by this time the one hundred and ninety-nine steps back into town were much quieter. As he left the graveyard a new plaque on the church wall caught his attention, it read: "To the memory of Mary Linskill, Novelist 1840 – 1891 worshiper at this church". Matthews sighed, this had been an old friend of his mothers, he hadn't known that she too had died this year.

Matthews dragged his feet down the one hundred and ninety-nine steps, he was not in rush to get to his father's house. The shops were closed and the high street filled only with children playing and those still making their way home from church. He was already dreading small talk with his father and John, it was the last thing he could think of as being fun. He would rather go home and continue working on his case.

As he walked along Church Street wrapped in his thoughts, he suddenly realised that somebody was calling his name. He turned to see Mrs Sheppard shuffling up the cobbled road after him.

'Detective…Detective Matthews,' she shouted in a breathless holler.

'Is everything okay Mrs Sheppard?' She took hold of his arm to steady herself and took numerous deep breaths.

'I saw you pass my window, I was hoping to see you. I was planning to come to the station tomorrow, but since you are on the street. You don't mind me discussing the investigation on your day off do you?'

'Not at all Mrs Sheppard, what is it that has you

concerned?'

'I have something that might be of use to you, come back to the guest house and I will hand it to you.'

Matthews kept hold of her arm and helped her over the uneven road. He was curious as to what she could possibly have of interest.

CHAPTER 15

Mrs Sheppard led Matthews into her guest house and directed him towards the sitting room. As he had expected it was extremely floral and had numerous arm chairs of all different sizes and patterns. It was certainly designed to be a communal area for her guests to sit and relax.

'Please take a seat detective. Would you like a cup of tea, I just made a pot?'

'That would be lovely, thank you.'

Matthews waited for her to return, he didn't feel

in much of a rush as the longer it took the more time he didn't have to spend with his family waiting for the Sunday roast to be served. The sitting room had numerous frames on every available surface with different black and white photographs. There was a stylish clock on the fire place which ticked loudly, and the window which looked out onto Church Street had a net up for privacy although you could still hear people passing by clearly.

'I am so pleased I saw you passing,' said Mrs Sheppard as she re-entered the sitting room, carrying a tray of cups and a teapot, 'saves me a journey up to the station tomorrow.'

Matthews smiled and cleared some of the frames from the coffee table so she could place the tray down. She poured them both a cup, offering milk and sugar to which he accepted, before sitting down in one of the large arm chairs with her own cup.

'Is the investigation going well detective?' she asked before taking a sip of her tea, she too was clearly in no hurry and spoke to the detective as though he had called around for a social visit.

'I have a couple of leads Mrs Sheppard, but still a way to go. Did you say you had something for me?' He tried not to sound rude but he also didn't want to be sipping tea all afternoon with her either.

'Yes detective. A letter arrived yesterday morning for Mr Robinson, and…well you see since he has died I thought you might want it?'

'Yes I can take a look, I found a box full in his room, which I have taken already so I will add it to the pile. I haven't found too much out from the letters yet but I am still reading through them.'

Mrs Sheppard put down her cup and stood, reached over to the large wooden side table and opened one of the draws where she pulled out the letter and she turned and handed it to the detective.

'Also detective I was wondering if I would be able to clean up Mr Robinson's room and rent it out again. I daren't do it until I had spoken to you.' Her hands shook slightly as she picked up the cup once again. Matthews thought she was going to spill her tea all down herself, but she managed to steady it again and continue drinking.

'Mrs Sheppard is everything okay, you look nervous?'

'Oh lad…sorry, I mean detective, I had a young man shouting at me on the door step last night. Still a little shaken up but I will be okay.' She buried her face into her cup and enjoyed her hot drink.

'Do you know who this man was, or what he wanted?'

'He wasn't really wanting me, he wanted Mr Robinson. Said he owed him money, and didn't believe me when I told him he had died, he started shouting at me, saying I was protecting him.'

'Can you describe this man, or did he give any indication who he was?'

'He didn't say, but he would have been in his late forties, maybe early fifties. He had a short beard, dark but greying, just like his hair really. Large in build, clearly sent to scare Mr Robinson as he was much broader than he was.' Matthews scribbled down what she had told him, he wondered if it was one of the people on his list to look into. He knew of at least two people James Robinson owed money to thanks to the woman in the bar's information.

'Mrs Sheppard if this man comes back, or anybody comes calling for Mr Robinson, please tell them to come and see me at the station. But if anybody starts being intimidating to you please let me know okay.' He was genuinely concerned about her, she looked white as a sheet and on edge.

'Thank you detective, you are most kind. Now about the room, may I clean it out and re-use it?'

'Could I have one more look around now before you do, just in case I missed anything?'

'Of course detective, feel free to go right ahead.' They finished their drinks and Mrs Sheppard handed Matthews the key to the room. He didn't expect to find anything but knew it was best to check. Upon entering the room he noticed that it appeared exactly as he had left it. He again searched through the bed side table, and wardrobe. He looked under the bed and even through the pockets of his clothes.

He had in his hand the letter Mrs Sheppard had given him, and curiously he decided to open it.

There was no indication on the envelope as to where it had come from, and the well written handwriting on the front gave very little away. He pulled out the paper within and sat on the bed to read it. As he sat on the bed, he heard a rustling noise come from underneath. He stood, pulled back the bedding that he had already checked through only to reveal nothing there. He placed the letter on the side table and then began to fully unmake the bed, pulling off the sheets to reveal the bare mattress, still nothing. He lifted the mattress to reveal the bed frame, still nothing. However, as he lifted the mattress he saw a small cut in the stitching which looked out of place. He prised it open slightly only for the entire stitching to come undone to reveal hidden within the mattress a number of objects, which he instantly reached in and pulled out. Inside the mattress he found an envelope filled with money and a piece of paper with a name and address on, a bag of white powder, which Matthews instantly recognised as coca. Finally, there was a brown paper bag which concealed a pistol.

Shocked by his new discovery Matthews began to re-check all the furniture in case Mr Robinson had hidden anything else in a cunning way, but he did not find anything further. He reverted his attention back to the letter, the paper and handwriting combined he recognised as having numerous letters from this person already to go through. He sat back on the bed and read.

My dear son, your wife has given birth to a healthy baby girl. She is a blessing from god and you should come home at once to meet her. Stop this nonsense and come home to your family.

WB.

This was the first time Matthews had seen these letters give any indication of who they were from, and being from his father made sense given the content of the others. What struck him about this letter though was it did not say 'you have become a father,' it simply stated his wife had had a baby. Was he thinking too much of this, was it a mere slip, or was the baby not his? How long exactly had Mr Robinson been away from her exactly, he wondered?

He then leaned over to the envelope of money

and pulled out the piece of paper within. It said "Jackson, Nibley, Bristol". He presumed Jackson was the surname of somebody, and possibly that Nibley was a place near Bristol, but he couldn't be certain.

Matthews collected up the items and straightened up the bed before leaving. Mrs Sheppard heard him coming back downstairs and offered him another cup of tea as he handed her back the room key.

'No thank you. I really should get going, I am expected for dinner.'

'Okay detective, well enjoy yourself.'

'Before I go Mrs Sheppard, I don't suppose you ever heard Mr Robinson making enquiries about anybody around town do you, as though he was looking for somebody?'

'I know when he first arrived, he asked me if I knew somebody, but it was so long ago detective I can't remember what name he mentioned now.'

'Was it Jackson by any chance?' She paused for a moment to think, but began to shake her head as she struggled to recall. 'Don't worry Mrs Sheppard, it's okay. If you do think of anything else that may help my investigation, please come and see me at the station.'

'Thank you detective, I will do that.'

CHAPTER 16

It was Monday morning, and Detective Matthews was exhausted. He had spent a great deal of the night reading all the remaining letters of James Robinson's. The ones he now knew to be from this father didn't really give him anything more than general family updates and more pleads to come home. A number of letters he figured came from his wife, her pleading with him to come home was basically the running theme throughout, but little more than that. Finally, there was a letter written by somebody else, but it was not signed, nor was it in an envelope, it simply sat in the small box underneath all of the others, it read.

James, I have managed to locate him to Whitby on the North Yorkshire coast. He is apparently living with family up there but I have yet to find out their names or address. If you want me to keep searching you will need to pay more money. B.

Matthews already knew James was looking for somebody whilst in Whitby, his co-worker had mentioned that already; but this letter was now solid proof. What he needed to figure out was who he was looking for, and if that is what ultimately led to his death. Matthews did however already have a couple of names to look into that he now knew James owed money to, and his intention this morning was to go to the station and look into these names, with the hope of locating them and speaking face to face as soon as possible.

There was a knock on the door at eight, and Harvey was their waiting with the horses and carriage in the sun filled street to collect him.

'G'morning sir,' he greeted in his usual cheer, 'blue skies already, should be a nice day.'

'Good morning Harvey, please come in I am not

quite ready.' Harvey entered Matthews house and followed him through into the kitchen where Matthews had laid out on the table his bag, his notepad and the new evidence he had taken from the guesthouse.

'Cor… what's all this sir?'

'Evidence from the victim's bedroom at the guesthouse, I did another search there yesterday. He had all of this hidden inside the mattress.' Harvey gasped at the detective's words, 'We need to get straight to the station so I can log these.' He started putting the items in his leather bag, a tight squeeze for it all but he managed it.

'Detective I have been told to tell ya that the coroner wishes to see you this morning. He has finished his report on the body.'

'But I asked him to send the report to the station directly.'

'Apparently he has asked to see you in person sir, clearly something he wishes to discuss with you face-to-face.'

'Fine,' Matthews sighed, 'we will go their first just in case he has something for me to take away, and then straight to the station.'

'Also sir, I didn't see or hear anything more with Grace yesterday. I'm sorry.'

'You don't need to apologies, now come on we need to leave.'

Matthews followed Harvey out of the door and to the carriage, where Harvey held the door open for the detective.

During the ride to the coroner Matthews watched from the window as shops were opening throughout the town. He had been away from Whitby for over five years, the first three being a junior officer in the town of Malton before moving to York. Yet somehow being back these past couple of days made him feel as though he had never been away at all. He didn't dislike being back in Whitby as much as he thought he would, although he still resented his father for going behind his back.

'We are here sir,' Harvey called from the front as they came to a halt. Matthews took his bag containing all his evidence with him, he dare not let it out of his sight until it was safely at the station. They had parked at the end of the narrow alley, and the detective walked the last few hundred yards to the coroner's door, knocking loudly he was keen to get away as soon as possible.

'Good morning detective,' Mr Waters greeted in the doorway, 'an early start this morning I see.' The elderly man beckoned him inside.

'Good morning Mr Waters, I hope you are well. Tell me is there a reason you needed me to collect this in person, I was under the impression you were sending your report directly to the station.' He tried not to sound rude, but he didn't see the need for this meeting.

'Detective, I want to show you a couple of things I have found,' he led him into the large room they had been in before. Laid on the table, covered in a sheet up to his neck, was James Robinson's body. 'I have the report here detective,' he handed Matthews a written report sealed in an envelope, 'but I need to explain a couple of things I have learnt. Firstly, the wooden branches and twigs that were strapped to his wrists, well they were tide so tightly that they caused small injuries to his wrists. However, the contraption was not strong enough to keep him held down, not by his own strength and not by the tide. So this suggests he was either already dead or unconscious when tied up.'

'I have since learnt Mr Waters that the contraption is known as a penny hedge, and is made as a ceremonial thing. It is only supposed to last three tides before being washed away.'

'Ah, that makes sense. I have heard of one of those. Didn't realise people still went on with that tradition; but here we are.'

'But if it did not tie him down Mr Waters then what was the purpose of tying the victim to it, and why didn't it wash away?'

'Perhaps the person who did it thought that it would tie him down long enough for him to drown, and I believe the reason it did not wash away was because it was tied so tightly to his wrists, that it was being more useful as handcuffs than its supposed use.' Mr Waters suddenly gave a retching couch as though phlegm was caught in his throat. He looked old and frail himself.

'But you sent me a letter the other day saying Mr Robinson had indeed died from drowning. How can that be if the penny hedge didn't keep him anchored down?'

'Well detective, that is my next finding. You see his lungs were filled with salt water, suggesting he was certainly alive and breathing when he reached the beach. I did a few more tests and found alcohol in him, quite a lot, so I can quite confidently say he was extremely intoxicated. Although being drunk can of course lead to drowning, the fact his hands were tied implies foul play, so I did a number of other checks.'

'What kind of checks?'

'Alcohol consumption can easily lead to drowning, but I don't believe that Mr Robinson could have been tied to the beach having only been drunk. When I looked into his stomach I found a half dissolved pill still in there. It had not fully made it to the stomach which means that he had taken it shortly before dying.'

'What kind of pill?' Matthews knowledge on drugs was minimal.

'I compared it to a number of over the counter drugs, and I believe it to be codeine, which is an opioid drug. It is generally used for pain relief but when mixed with alcohol can have a serious effect. The effects of a high dose, especially with such volumes of alcohol means the side effects would not have taken long to kick in. Unofficially I believe that whilst his body was shutting down he somehow ended up on the beach. Although he was still alive when the tide came in I think he was probably almost dead anyway, the sea simply made sure of the job.'

'So Mr Waters, do you think whoever put him on the beach gave him the drugs?

'I couldn't say for certain. He could of course taken them himself unknowing of the danger. As I mentioned this is an over the counter drug, so easily accessible to anybody.'

'Thank you Mr Waters, I presume all of this is in

the report?'

'Yes detective. However, the reason I asked to see you in person today is because my report simply states what I found in his stomach, a clinical report, I wanted to explain to you exactly what that means in terms of his death. His hands tied shows he was more than likely murdered, but the drugs in his stomach cannot be full on proof that he took them himself or not. Nor can I one hundred per cent prove how much of the drug he ingested, I just wished to explain to you my theory.'

'Thank you Mr Waters, I appreciate your time. I am starting to piece together quite a lot of information about Mr Robinson now.'

CHAPTER 17

When Detective Matthews finally made it into the office Mrs Lloyd-Hughes was already at her desk typing away at her typewriter; a cigarette dangling between her lips as she typed. She gave a friendly nod to the detective as he entered her office on route to his own.

'Would you come into my office Mrs Lloyd-Hughes when you have a moment, there are a couple of things I would like you to do for me when you have time.' She gave a crooked smile, trying not to drop the cigarette, and nodded to acknowledge his words whilst continuing to type.

In his office, Matthews was pleased to see a little more furniture had now been added, his father's doing no doubt. He now had a typewriter and oil burning lamp on his desk so he could work when it got dark. A carved wooden framed sofa with tapestry upholstery now sat against the wall, and an ugly Persian rug sat in the centre of the office in front of his large desk. There was also a plant in the window, a number of books on the once bare shelves and his desk draws had been filled with stationary.

Matthews unpacked his evidence onto his desk to look at it, and scanned through his notebook for the names of the men who James Robinson owed money. He knew at least one of these gangs had been seen close to him on the night he had died, and needed to find out more about what happened outside the pub.

A gentle knock on the door and a croaky, 'Y-You wished to s-see me detective' came from the doorway, followed by an almighty cough.

'Ah yes, Mrs Lloyd-Hughes, come in and take a seat; this won't take long.' She did as she was told and took one of the wooden chairs opposite him; the now cluttered desk between them. 'As you know I am working on the James Robinson case, and I have two names I need looking up so I can locate them and question them about their whereabouts that evening. Given what I know about them already they will undoubtedly have a file.'

'N-No problem sir, if you t-tell me the names I will check the police files today.'

'The first one is Johnny King,' she scribbled down the name on a notepad, Matthews hadn't even seen her bring it in, 'and the second is Damian Campbell.' She did not write the second name down and instead looked at the detective and smiled as though she knew something he didn't.

'S-Sir you will find Damian Campbell at the Duke of York public house bar,' she croaked before raging into yet another coughing fit. Matthews waited patiently for her to finish. 'H-He is the landlord there.'

'Really? The landlord, I was not expecting that. Do we have a file on him at all?'

'Oh yes sir, quite a c-character indeed. His close acquaintances refer to him as DC. H-He's been in prison a number of times over the years, but only short stays.' She cleared her throat before continuing. 'He's mostly known in town for g-generally throwing his weight around and getting into c-conflicts, but has also been in trouble for hosting illegal gambling nights after hours. He's never been convicted for anything like murder, but rumour has it he will give anybody who owes him money a good beating to an inch of their life.'

'So how come his convictions for assault haven't landed him away for longer?'

'N-Nobody will t-testify, so if and when caught there is very little the judge can do without a s-solid statement.' Matthews could hear her voice was getting worse, and between its usual croak and smokers cough she was becoming more difficult to understand. 'M-Most people who deal with him know that even with him locked away he has security at the Duke that are basically his muscles, and extremely ruthless as he is, n-nobody dare testify against him because they know his team will come after them.'

'Why on Earth would a pub need security?' Matthews asked her, making his own notes now.

'T-That's just the title he gives them, we all know they are more his hit men, but you cannot convict somebody for having security and without proof it's difficult to bring him down.'

'Well he is one of two potential leads I have, I know Mr Robinson owed Damian Campbell money so I need to speak with him. I will go this afternoon before the bar gets too busy,' said Matthews, feeling less than happy at the prospect.

'I am also wanting to locate a lady that goes by the name of Ellen Garner. Apparently, she lives on the west coast somewhere and is known to have been having intimate relations with Mr Robinson. He was seen headed in the opposite direction to the guest house he was staying, so he could have been headed her way. We know his body was on the west cliff side of town, so he clearly crossed the bridge at some point. So maybe he was going to her house, I'll need to speak with her and check.' Mrs Lloyd-

Hughes nodded and scribbled down the name.

'It is p-possible she won't be on file sir if she doesn't have a record, s-so it may take some time for me to ask around.'

'Thank you Mrs Lloyd-Hughes. Also, I have these items which I took from the victims bedroom at Mrs Sheppard's guest house, do we have a safe I can lock them away in whilst I am out?' Matthews felt quite strange being new to the station again despite him knowing the place so well. He was still finding it funny being referred to as detective and sir and had to stop himself from smirking.

'Yes sir, s-safe's just behind my desk.' She said this as she rose to her feet, presuming their meeting was over. Matthews smirked in amusement.

'Before you go, do you know anybody by the surname Jackson?'

'Jackson?' she repeated, pursing her lips as she thought. 'It's a common name but I don't think so detective, w-why do you ask?'

'I believe Mr Robinson was in Whitby looking

for somebody, I believe it could be somebody with that surname.'

'I'll have a look to see if we have anybody on file with that name too sir,' she scribble on her pad, 'but I d-don't know of a family with than name personally. Will that be all, sir?' Matthews thanked her as she shuffled out of his office in yet another coughing fit, moments later the sound of her typewriter tapping away started up again.

Matthews continued flicking through his notepad, and also read the coroner's report. It was exactly as he had explained it, minus his own personal thoughts that were not solid enough evidence to include. He was stalling going to see Damian Campbell, and was even contemplating whether taking another officer for backup was necessary. He also remembered the pistol locked away in his desk and wondered whether it would be wise to carry it with him.

He spent the remainder of the morning typing up his notes, and made a timeline of James Robinson's actions the night he died. It still had some way to go but Matthews could see pieces already starting to come together. As he finished going through his notes, and was about to collect up all the items to take to the safe, there was another knock on his door; this time much louder and the visitor did not wait to be invited in.

'Ah here you are at last Benjamin, I was concerned when I didn't see you first thing.' It was Matthews father, the chief of police.

'I went straight to the coroner's office before coming in, for the report on James Robinson; and please don't refer to me by my first name…Pops, you don't do it with the other officers and detectives.' He emphasised his use of the name Pops, the name he had always called his father, and hoped the irony was not wasted on him.

'Still not a Monday morning person I see, grumpy as always. Well never mind it is pretty much lunchtime so go eat something; that usually perks you up.' He let out a belly aching laugh which caused his entire body to shake, and the sound of his laughter echoed down the corridor.

'I was actually about to head out again to follow

up some leads I have.'

'Well before you go give me a brief update on what you have so far son.' Matthews looked at his father with displeasure, he knew he wouldn't be able to stop himself from constantly referring to him as his son instead of just a colleague. Through gritted teeth Matthews spoke through his notes quickly, explained the evidence laid out on his desk, and finally told him his plan on going to see Damian Campbell and hopefully the other man he knew Mr Robinson owed money to.

'Sounds like you have achieved quite a lot in just a short time so...' he stopped himself from saying son again. 'Still a way to go though. How is young Harvey doing, promising young lad if you ask me, certainly keen to be an officer one day.'

'Yes, he's fine, I can't complain for the assistance.'

'Well I better let you get on...detective.' He smirked at his own words. 'Keep me up to date with progress, and if you need anything you know where I am.'

Matthews put his head in his hands and leaned over his desk for a minute trying to suppress his annoyance at his father. After a couple of minutes he rose from his desk and walked over to his office window. He had the perfect view of the police stables and could see Harvey sweeping the yard. He opened the window and leaned out, already catching Harvey's attention before saying anything.

'Meet me out front in five minutes,' he shouted down to him, 'no horses this time, we are going to take a walk, and where we are going I think would be better suited not to have a police carriage parked up outside.'

CHAPTER 18

Harvey was stood on the front steps of the station waiting for the detective for a couple of minutes before Matthews finally emerged. He had with him his small leather briefcase containing his notepad and pencil drawing of Mr Robinson. Harvey on the other hand had nothing with him, and felt somewhat empty without his horses. They walked out of the yard in silence before Harvey finally spoke.

'Where are we headed detective?'

'We're going to see a Mr Damian Campbell, he is the landlord of the Duke of York pub. I have been informed that our Mr Robinson was in his debt, so I want to check out Mr Campbell's whereabouts that night.'

'Ah, I see,' Harvey mumbled, 'and why are we walking instead of taking the carriage?'

'Mr Campbell is quite well known for being on the wrong side of the law, and I don't think he will take kindly to me coming and questioning him; and I certainly don't think he will take kindly to a police vehicle being parked outside his pub. So better to not advertise our visit to the locals otherwise that might make him less likely to co-operate.'

'That makes sense sir,' he replied, just as his stomach made an almightily loud rumble.

'Have you eaten yet today lad?'

'Not since breakfast sir.'

'Me either, let's make a flying visit for something first.'

It was a pleasant walk into the town, Harvey talking most of the way. He told Matthews about his wishes to become a police officer, and how honoured he was that the chief allowed him to assist Matthews and be able to see an investigation first hand. He also spoke about how he had not known his own father and that the chief was the closest thing he had. For Matthews, this walk seemed to last much longer than he had anticipated.

They headed for the harbour bridge, which was currently opened to allow boats to pass; meaning the road leading up to it was filled with people and horse and carts all waiting to cross. The harbour was bustling and sounds and smells of the town seemed to be at their most prominent. Seagulls called overhead like an irritating alarm, dock workers were shouting loudly to one and other as they loaded and unloaded boats nearby. When the bridge finally closed and reopened to the road, Harvey had to duck and dive between a whole army of people and carriages that were crossing the bridge at the same time; and with a whole bunch of people coming from the other side too, it was chaos.

Matthews led Harvey over the bridge and around the corner to Sleightholme family bakery, an old favourite of his when he used to live in the town. It was only a small little white building, and Matthews needed to watch his head as he entered through the tiny door. Inside the small shop were multiple counters displaying loafs of freshly baked bread, a counter dedicated to a variety of cakes, another counter filled with fresh pastries and tray bakes. The entire bakery smelt delicious and had both Matthews and Harvey salivating within seconds.

'Benjamin Matthews. Well if my eyes don't deceive me, is that really you?' A young woman beamed with delight at seeing him and raced around the counted to greet him with a hug. 'What are you doing in town?' She was not very tall, but had long dark hair that was tied up into a hair net. Her eyes were large on her petite face and her smile lit up the room.

'Good afternoon Mary, it is great to see you again.' He said trying to breathe through the tight hug. 'Have you not heard I am back and now working as a detective for the station?'

'Oh I see,' she replied, returning back behind the counter, 'I didn't think I'd see the day you came back to Whitby permanently.' She gave out a sly grin as though she was secretly pleased.

'Well you can thank my father for that, you know what he is like for meddling.' They both laughed and nodded at this remark.

'Who's the kid?' asked Mary, as though only just realising he was stood there.

'Harvey, please meet Mary Sleightholme an old friend of mine. Harvey here works in the police stables but it hoping to be an officer one day.'

'Nice to meet you miss.' Harvey came forward and shook her hand across the high counter. She smirked and returned the pleasantries before turning her attention back to Matthews.

'If you like we could have a drink together sometime, you know, to toast your new job and welcome you back to town?' Her cheeks flushed pink as she said this.

'Sure, why not,' he replied. 'I am currently in the middle of quite a heavy going case, so I'll arrange something with you once it is over. Which reminds me, we need to be going.'

He purchased himself and Harvey a sweet pastry for the road, and even got them both some soft warm bread to eat now.

'I used to always be in here,' he told Harvey as they left, 'buying the crusty bread and pastries, and my goodness they are as good as I remember them. This bread is so tasty that when warm out of the oven it doesn't even need anything on it, I can just eat it plain.'

Neither of them talked as they walked along Church Street eating. A couple of homeless children chased after them. They were clearly no older than five or six, but they were so dirty and thin. Matthews handed what was left of his bread to them to share, and after seeing the kind gesture Harvey decided to do the same. Both children almost cried with delight at the gift, and hugged the detective's legs before running out of sight into one of the narrow alleys.

They continued along Church Street, which was just as busy with workers going about their business, and Matthews and Harvey had to swerve in and out of the way of oncoming people, horses and carts.

They were now on their way to the Duke of York pub to see Damian Campbell, and although Matthews had never met him before he was already a little intimidated by what Mrs Lloyd-Hughes had told him in his office.

As Church Street narrowed the further they went, they had to walk up against the buildings on one side to avoid the constant stream of horses and carts trying to get by in either direction. 'Another good reason not to bring the carriage.' Matthews remarked back to Harvey who was following behind. They continued walking along the street that was filled with people and just up ahead a lady dropped a hat box and a beautiful blue hat fell out onto the street. Matthews instantly recognised it was Grace and raced over to help her. She looked at him with slight annoyance and embarrassment as he picked up her box whilst she lifted the hat back inside.

'We just keep bumping into each other don't we detective.' She said taking the box from him.

'Are you okay Grace? Please let me know if anything is damaged and I will pay for it.' Despite this she avoided eye contact with the detective and made to leave without checking the contents of the box.

'No harm done, good day.' She tried to squeeze past him but a carriage was passing at that very moment trapping her in front of him. The bruise on her face from the other day was still clear, even if she had put on make-up to try and cover it over. The carriage seemed to take forever to pass, and although Matthews did not mind being trapped next to Grace for a couple of seconds, she looked slightly uncomfortable by it and kept her eye gaze down.

'My apologies if I over stepped the mark last time we spoke,' Matthews whispered to her in a soft tone, 'I did not mean to offend you Grace.' She sighed at his remark before her face finally softened.

'It's okay detective, I appreciate your concern. Good day.' The carriage had moved and so Grace was able to now pass them with ease.

'Stay here.' Matthews ordered Harvey before going after her. 'Grace,' he called, but she ignored and continued walking. He caught up to her easily and walked alongside her as he spoke. 'Grace please hear me out, I simply wish to know you are okay and safe. If he is hurting you then I beg you to…'

'Detective we have had this discussion before, and I will say this for the last time. My fiancé and I are happily in love and we will be married in August. I ask you not to interfere with us again.' Matthews jumped in front of her so she had no choice but to stop.

'Grace I cannot stop thinking about you, and it kills me to know what he is like. Just say the word and I can have him arrested, please for your own safety.'

'Goodbye detective.' She walked around him, and he decided that he had pushed it far enough and watched her as she marched along the street.

He returned to Harvey who was standing exactly where he had left him, and together they continued up the road to the Duke of York which was situated at the end of the street.

The Duke of York pub was currently closed, and did not open on a Monday until the early evening.

Matthews gave a loud knock on the door in the hope that somebody might be inside, and sure enough a minute later the door was unlocked and a large man stared at them from within.

'Well?' he said in a gruff voice. He was much taller than Matthews and his entire body was wider than the door frame. He was clean shaven and wore a dark suit, and his expression was certainly not of a welcoming nature.

'I was wondering if Mr Campbell was in, and if he had a moment to talk?' Matthews tried to sound authoritative but felt his voice sounded much higher and weaker than this giant of a man's.

'Who's asking?'

'My name is Detective Matthews, and I am in the middle of an investigation regarding the murder of a Mr James Robinson. I believe my victim was in Mr Campbell debt and I wanted to speak with him to find out any information Mr Campbell may know about this man.' The giant man hesitated for a moment, before opening the door wider and beckoning them inside.

'Sit there.'

He hollered once inside the bar area, and pointed to the table closest to the door. Matthews and Harvey did as they were told and waited as the giant man left the room. Matthews was starting to think that coming here unarmed, and without back up might have been the biggest mistake of his life.

CHAPTER 19

Detective Matthews and Harvey sat in the darkened bar for what felt like a long time, neither of them talking as they waited. Eventually voices came from the next room, and they did not sound happy. Matthews had dealt with criminals before, but he was more feeling guilty for putting Harvey through this than himself.

'Detective Matthews I presume?' A tall skinny man walked through the door, not at all the criminal looking thug Matthews was expecting. In fact, Damian Campbell was well dressed in a casual suit, had tidy hair and moustache and spoke rather sophisticatedly and soft. He pulled out the chair opposite the two men and sat, pulling out a metal case of cigars and after placing one in his own mouth turned the box around so as to offer the detective one. Matthews obliged and Campbell lit his own before holding out the lit match for Matthews to light his on. It all felt a little friendly for the detectives liking.

'Mr Campbell I am here…'

'I know why you are here detective; my doorman re-laid the entire story. What I want to know is what you think it has to do with me?' His voice remained calm and elegant, yet his words had a venom behind them.

'Mr Campbell I am trying to get a profile together of James Robinson, there seems to be little known about him, and I have been given the task of solving his case.' Matthews had to stop himself from raising his voice, he didn't know why but he already didn't like Mr Campbell. 'I have been informed that Mr Robinson did not have very many friends in town, and certainly knew how to make enemies. What I need from you is any information you may know about his whereabouts last week, and if you know anything relating to his murder?'

Damian Campbell let out a small chuckle. 'You certainly have your father's fire detective. He too struggles to keep his feelings hidden.' Matthews felt his face fluster as he tried to remain calm at this comment. 'But I will tell you this detective. James Robinson has been barred from my pub for over two months now, mostly for causing trouble, but also because he thinks he can gamble in my pub without paying out his losings. It wasn't me he lost the money to, but stupidly I paid off his losing's to one of my regulars so I wouldn't lose the business; that left his debt with me of more than fifty pounds. It is not my fault if he does not make that in a year, he should learn only to play within his means.' He took a drag on his cigar and slowly blew out the smoke.

'If he was banned from your pub Mr Campbell then did you ever go looking for him yourself for the payments.'

'He was never a difficult man to find, detective. He only lived at one of the guesthouses down the street, and I paid him a visit once or twice, but each time he claimed he didn't have my money.'

'Did you or any of your men ever physically harm him, to threaten him to pay?'

'Mr Robinson had a very short temper detective, and he was easy to unsettle. We may have, on occasion, irritated him in other bars in order to get him started in another fight. Thanks to my men he has now been barred from almost every pub in Whitby. I find that a more useful tool for somebody like him who enjoys going out drinking.' The more Matthews listened to him, the more he sounded like a snake.

'On the night of Wednesday sixth May did you order any of your men to pay him a visit?'

'No.'

'Did you personally see Mr Robinson?'

'No.'

'Can you recall the last time you saw him, or your men saw him?'

'Weeks ago. I have better things to do, *detective*,

than chase a lowlife like James Robinson around town for money he ain't going to pay me. I won't act surprised that he is dead, thugs like him always get their comeuppance eventually.'

'Mr Campbell are you aware of anybody else Mr Robinson may be affiliated with, somebody who may wish him dead?'

'I have no interest in his personal affairs detective, I barely knew the man and can honestly say that I have no feelings about what happened, nor do I know anything about it. So, if we are finished here I'm sure you wouldn't mind showing yourself out.'

He stood and turned his back on Matthews and Harvey and walked back out of the room through the door he had arrived. Deflated and a little angry, Matthews led Harvey back out onto the street in silence, both of them reframing from speaking until they were a safe distance away from the building.

'Do you think he is lying?' asked Harvey, as they headed back along the hustle and bustle of Church Street. Matthews grabbed him by the shoulder and led him into one of the many narrow alleys that led off of Church Street. Before speaking to the young lad he peered back around the corner checking that they were not being followed. He couldn't see Mr Campbell's men anywhere, but had a sneaking suspicion he would now be on their watch list. He turned back to Harvey to answer his question.

'The prostitute in the pub told me she saw his thugs headed for James Robinson shortly after he was thrown out of the Black Horse Inn,' he whispered, 'she said they often gave him a beating and she went inside to avoid watching it. Although she never confirmed he was beaten I find it difficult to believe that they would simply walk past him. She also mentioned that he apparently staggered off extremely drunk in the opposite direction to where he lived.'

'So he *is* lying.'

'Yes, at least that he and his men had not seen him in weeks. Mr Campbell was rather confident about himself, especially when it came to saying he knew nothing about the murder. He is either an extremely good actor or he has no knowledge of what happened.'

'How so?'

'Well of course his men could have been sent to beat up Mr Robinson on Campbell's orders, or perhaps they just happened to see him outside the Black Horse Inn and decided to act off their own initiative.'

'Meaning Campbell wouldn't necessarily know about the fight?' Harvey concluded.

'Exactly. But given Mr Campbell's status, even if he didn't order the fight, I can't believe that his men wouldn't tell him afterwards. You know, almost gloating about what they'd done.'

'So you think it was them who killed him then?'

'If Mr Robinson's body had been found dumped normally, I would say I am more inclined to lean that way, but given the fact he was tied up in Mrs Hutton's penny hedge on the beach leads me to hesitate. If all of his men are like the one we met, they hardly need a flimsy bit of twigs to tie him down; unless...' He trailed off into his own thoughts.

'Unless what detective?'

'Unless they saw the penny hedge and decided to make it look like somebody else. What I really need to do is speak to one or two of his so-called security guards alone, they are probably less cool under pressure than Mr Campbell.'

'How do you expect to do that, sir?'

'I don't know Harvey, but I think a night trip back to Church Street may be in order in the hope to see them prowling. I'm hopeful that tomorrow Mrs Lloyd-Hughes will have the address of Johnny King so we can question him, and maybe after that we can start narrowing down what we have.'

Matthews dismissed Harvey for the rest of the day, it was now late afternoon and Matthews was exhausted. He headed home where he intended to write up notes of his conversation with Campbell.

Upon reaching his house Matthews fumbled with his keys in the door, and before he could put it in the lock the door burst open in front of him, his sister Charlotte met him in his doorway.

'I wondered what time you would be getting home,' she greeted him with a hug, 'I've put a pie in your oven that I baked this afternoon. I'm sure you're not eating much living alone.'

'Lotty I'm fine, please don't worry about me.' He followed her through to the kitchen and she couldn't control her excitement at showing him the pie.

'Mothers recipe, she left me all her old recipe cards.' She thrust the pie excitedly under his nose so he could smell it.

'That's great Lotty, now if you don't mind I need to write up some notes from my day.' She slammed down the pie in displeasure and sighed loudly at him. 'Lotty, please don't be like that, I appreciate the pie, I really do. You are more than welcome to stay but please just let me scribble down some notes before I forget what is in my head.'

'Okay, well I will warm up the pie and we can have it together. I want to tell you all about what John and I are planning for our wedding.' Matthews forced a smile and took out his notebook to make his notes. He loved his sister more than anything, but tonight he wished for nothing more than peace and quiet.

His note taking didn't last long at all, and as he was placing the pad back into his bag there was a knock on the door. Charlotte raced to answer it and to Matthews surprise it was his father, carrying two bottles of wine.

'We never really did toast your new job and house did we Benji, so get some glasses out lad, and Lotty serve us all some of that pie.' His voice was so loud it echoed up the staircase as he walked through to the kitchen, slamming the wine bottles down on the table and looking overly pleased with himself. 'I promise not to talk work tonight, *detective*.' He slapped his son on the back playfully and laughed, a bellowing howl of a laugh.

'Pops we really don't need to do this tonight, we can…'

'Nonsense son, any later and you will have lived here too long for a proper toast. Now come on, where are those glasses.'

Matthews fetched the glasses whilst his sister heated and then sliced up the pie. He had to admit it was kind of nice having a meal with them both in his own place, even if it did seem strange it happening to be his grandmother's old kitchen.

His father kept his word and they did not speak about work at all. Instead, Lotty told them about her wedding plans which she was planning for later in the year. They also talked about their mother and told old stories that made them laugh, as well as old funny stories about their grandmother's house. It turned out to be a pleasant evening after all. When his father and sister made to leave, they were pleasantly surprised to see that it was already after ten, the time had just flown by.

'Oh, I nearly forgot to give you this.' His father said as he stepped out of the door. It was an envelope. 'Mrs Lloyd-Hughes found the address of the man you wished to question, I told her I was seeing you so would pass it on. Technically, I am over the threshold and have left now, so can talk work again.' He laughed, and his entire body shook as he and Charlotte walked down the front steps into the street.

Matthews did not reply to his father regarding the case and simply wished them both 'goodnight' before closing the door. He ripped open the envelope and inspected its content. It read in Mrs Lloyd-Hughes neat handwriting:

Johnny King, 17 John Street. Previous convictions related to drug dealing and money laundering.

Matthews knew where John Street was, it was the street leading off of Havelock Place. Could that be yet another coincidence, he wondered.

CHAPTER 20

etective Matthews woke to the sound of somebody banging on his door. He reached over to his bedside table, which had a candlestick holder with a half melted white candle attached, a box of matches and an empty mug which had contained tea. Matthews stretched passed these objects to reach his pocket watch, it read 8am. He was late.

Jumping out of his bed he raced to his window to see who was on his doorstep; it was Harvey. He quickly opened the window to tell Harvey he was headed down straight away, and threw on his shirt and trousers, which were laid out on a wooden chair waiting. He grabbed his waistcoat and watch and raced down the stairs to open the door.

'Morning detective,' said Harvey, 'sleep in did ya?'

'It would appear so, yes.' Matthews huffed as he buttoned up the remaining buttons of his shirt and led Harvey through into the kitchen. 'Have you eaten?'

'Yes sir, porridge.'

'Good, well take a seat I need something quick before we leave. I have Johnny King's address and it isn't far. What's that?'

'Newspaper sir, *Whitby gazette…*'

'Why do you have it?' Matthews asked before Harvey had the chance to explain.

'There's a piece in 'ere about you detective. Just a small something, underneath an advert for this years Regatta, but still I figured ya'd wanna know. Want me to read it ya whilst ya getting ready?'

'Go on then.' Matthews replied as he put a kettle

on the hob to boil. Harvey unfolded the paper, cleared his throat and began to read.

Whitby has a new detective in town, with the appointment of Benjamin Matthews to the force this week. The new detective, a twenty-four-year-old bachelor, is no stranger to the Whitby streets, or Police station for that matter, as he is known to be the chief of polices eldest son. No prizes then to guess how he managed to get the job. Reports suggest he is already working on the case of the beach murder reported last week. So only time will tell if the new Detective Matthews will shine in his new role, or lean back onto his father for support.

Matthews slammed down his cup on the counter, breaking off the handle. 'I knew people would see my returning here like this, I told the old fool I didn't want this bloody thing. I was happy in York. When this case is over, I am heading back there, it's much better to be a constable under my own merit than a detective under daddy.' Harvey folded the newspaper away.

'Sorry detective, I didn't mean to upset you, I just thought you would have wanted to know.'

'No need to apologise Harvey, not your fault at all. Thank you for telling me. Anyway would you like something to drink or anything?'

'No thank you sir, I am okay.' Matthews joined Harvey at the table as he enjoyed his warm drink, he needed to stop thinking about the newspaper article otherwise it was going to drive him crazy.

'Where did you learn to read so well, by the way?' He knew Harvey was an orphan, and by definition that usually led to no, or little schooling.

'I went to school for a little bit, but then mi Mam died and I had to go out and get work. Started on the docks I did but never enjoyed that, I always wanted to be a police officer, and so when I heard about the yard job I just knew it was for me. I live with mi grandmother now but she don't do much other than stay in bed all day; she can't walk you see.' Despite telling the detective all this Harvey maintained a positive tone throughout.

'Well I think your mother would be very proud to see the man you are becoming.' Harvey smiled with a hint of embarrassment, and Matthews too was starting to feel a little awkward. 'Time to go I think, Johnny King lives just a couple of streets away so hopefully he is in.'

After clearing away his cups and finishing getting ready, both Matthews and Harvey were outside by the horses and carriage in no time. He threw his bag, containing his notepad into the carriage, and after yawning multiple times already decided instead to walk the short journey alongside the horses. 'Hopefully the sea breeze and short stroll will wake me up.' He commented to Harvey who sat in his usual spot upon the carriage and guided the horses along the road. 'The last thing I want is to be yawning whilst questioning him.'

Matthews made the decision that the carriage should again stay out of sight in case Johnny King got upset by it, and instructed Harvey to leave the horses at the end of the street.

'Can I join you again detective?' he asked.

'You can join me to the front door, but I'd rather you stay outside and keep watch of the horses; it was irresponsible of me to put you in danger yesterday.' Harvey nodded and followed the detective up John Street until they got to number seventeen.

The street was lined with bricked terraced houses that were all three levels high, and had small bay windows and little railed fences out front. The front gardens of these houses were barely big enough for a handful of plant pots to sit in. The horses were all the way back down in front of number one, tied to the lamp post, and as the numbered houses passes Harvey started to get nervous again.

Matthews knocked on the door and waited, Harvey held back a couple of feet at the bottom of four stone steps that lead up to the door. There was no sound coming from inside. The bay window next to the front door had been blacked out so nobody could see inside. Matthews knocked again, this time louder. They waited and listened until eventually they could hear movement from inside. Matthews leaned into the door to try and hear what was going on, and as he was about to knock again the sound of the door being unlocked made him jump back.

'Can I help you?' A man's voice came out from the barely opened door. The door had clearly been put on a chain and the occupant could not be seen through the small opening.

'I was wondering if I could speak with a Mr Johnny King?' Matthews asked, his voice firm and clear.

'And who are you?' The disembodied voice was deep and slightly angry sounding.

'My name is Detective Matthews and…' Before Matthews could finish the man slammed the door shut and the sound of locks began to re-click into position. Matthews began to bang on the door again. 'Mr King please let me speak with you; I am trying to collect information on a Mr James Robinson who I believe owed you money.'

Matthews continued knocking on the door for several more minutes, he spoke loudly in the hope Mr King would open up again, but he never did. After five minutes he had to claim defeat.

'Do you think he knows something?' asked Harvey.

'I don't know, he slammed the door as soon as I mentioned I was a detective. I think he probably has something to hide in there but that doesn't mean it's connected to my case. He is a known drug dealer, and unfortunately I don't have any permission to enter or search his house yet; I was hoping a simple conversation would have been a good starting ground.'

'So what happens now?' queried Harvey as they made their way back to the carriage.

'Well we will have to go through everything else we have and see if we can solve the case without having to have a conversation with Mr King. I still need to speak with Mr Campbell's security, I think that is our main objective right now. I also need to find this Ellen Garner lady who was thought to be having intimate relations with Robinson, perhaps she knew a little more about him.'

'And Mr King?'

'Well if he won't open the door there is nothing I can do right now, but if evidence starts to point this way I will be able to use force, or even bring him into the station for questioning.' Harvey untied the horses from the lamp post and Matthews walked around him to get into the carriage. Upon entering the carriage the detective gasped.

'What is it detective?' Harvey enquired.

'My bag, it was on the seat in here. It's gone.'

CHAPTER 21

Matthews jumped back out of the carriage and scanned up and down the street, there was nobody around. He quickly got back inside and checked the floor in case the bag had fallen, but it was not there.

Deflated by this setback Matthews hopped back into the carriage, and Harvey drove the horses back to the police station. The entire journey Matthews could not stop thinking about his stolen bag, and wondered who could have done this. Maybe some kids playing a prank, he thought, or a citizen who dislikes the police causing a nuisance; or worse, it could be somebody linked to the case. Matthews had not even been a detective for a whole week yet, but he was sure that losing a notepad containing information on a murder case is a sackable offence. He spent the majority of the ride with his head in his hands. Completely fed up of the case, fed up of being in Whitby and fed up of his father's constant rule over him; he was certain that once this case was finished, he would be heading back to York with or without his father's blessing.

Upon arriving into the office Mrs Lloyd-Hughes was tapping away as usual at her typewriter, but stopped the moment Matthews walked in. She took the cigarette balanced between her lips down into a small dish and gave the detective a warm smile as he approached.

'G-Good morning detective, I have some paperwork here for you and I've also been able to locate an address for Ellen Garner.' She seemed chirpy, although her croaky voice seemed no better.

'Who?' questioned Matthews, mostly because he didn't fully hear her.

'Ellen Garner, s-sir. You know, the woman Mr

Robinson was thought to be having an intimate affair with.'

'Ah yes, I remember. When you have time today would you mind writing her a letter asking her to come to the station to speak with me, ideally tomorrow if she can.' He took the pile of papers that she was holding and thanked her. 'Also, I want to get all the evidence on the case back out of the safe, I need to go over my notes again.' He dare not tell her about his notepad being stolen. She told him to take a seat and that she would bring them through to him.

'D-Detective is everything okay?' She asked moments later carrying an armful of items. Matthews was slightly taken aback by her question; he wasn't sure if she was meaning personally or with the case.

'Yes,' he replied, watching her place the items out onto his desk. 'Thank you for bringing these through.'

'You're welcome, sir. A-Also I wished to tell you that the other surname you gave me, Jackson, came up blank. We don't have anybody on file with that surname. I did ask around too, but nobody knew anybody with that surname.' She took out her handkerchief and started another one of her coughing fits, thankfully though this one did not go on for too long.

'Curious,' Matthews sighed, 'I'm almost certain that James Robinson was looking for somebody with that surname, but he was clearly struggling. Something kept him in Whitby all this time and I don't think it was his job or high-class friends. He clearly thought this Jackson person was in or around town and was determined to find him.' Mrs Lloyd-Hughes nodded in agreement as the detective mumbled on, she was not fully certain if he was actually talking to her or just thinking out loud. 'Thank you Mrs Lloyd-Hughes, this is great.'

'If you do need anything else just let me know.' She left the office and returned to her desk. After another brief spurt of coughing a blue smoke cloud appeared near the office door signalling that she had resumed her cigarette, and a second later her typing continued.

Matthews looked through all of the notes he had typed up just the day before. He had always done this due to his appalling handwriting in his notebooks, and now with his bag being stolen he was doubly pleased he had them. He now had just two more witnesses left to speak with, Ellen Garner and the Duke of York security men. Having gotten nowhere with the Duke of York landlord Damian Campbell, Matthews knew he needed to speak with some of his men. They had been seen hanging around Church Street the night of his murder, and were certainly high on Matthews' list of potential suspects. His plan was to go out drinking this evening at the Black Horse Inn, with the hope that Damian Campbell's men were prowling the area as they are often known to be.

After reading through all of his typed notes Mrs Lloyd-Hughes knocked on his door and re-entered.

'Letter drafted for Ellen Garner, sir. Does this sound okay for what you wanted?' She slid the piece of paper across his desk and Matthews scanned his eyes across it.

Dear Mrs Garner.

We are currently following up leads on a recent murder in the Whitby area and believe you may have known the victim James Robinson. We are currently trying to create a profile for Mr Robinson and are looking to speak with anybody who knew him. Please would you consider coming into the police station tomorrow (Wednesday, May 13) at your own convenience.

Thank you very much for your co-operation in advance.

Kind Regards

Detective B. Matthews

'Thank you Mrs Lloyd-Hughes, I think this looks ideal. Please could we get this sent out as soon as possible? Feel free to ask Harvey to deliver it; he is always looking for something *policing* to do.' He chuckled at his own sarcasm.

'V-Very well, sir.' She retreated out of the office again and headed down the staircase at the end of the corridor with the letter.

Matthews returned to his pile of evidence and came across the items that were originally found in James Robinson's pocket by the coroner. His first bit of evidence during the case. All destroyed paper pieces that barely survived the sea water. There was the corner of the docks pay check, and the piece of paper with *Havelock Place* written on it. As he stared at the piece of paper with the street name on he couldn't help wonder what else was part of this note. Could it have given him the answers he needed? The residents of Havelock Place had all been questioned about James Robinson, and none of them claimed to know him; and with no evidence showing that any of them have a connection with him he had nothing to tie any of them in. Of course, the note could have been referring to somewhere near Havelock Place, or could even been a list of streets Mr Robinson was working his way through. Matthews knew Robinson was looking for somebody in Whitby and he could certainly have been searching by street name.

It then occurred to him that the writing on the piece of paper looked familiar. But of course it did, he had seen this paper already. But no, that wasn't it, something about this writing seemed all too familiar this time around, but what was it? He racked his brains trying to think what it was that could be niggling at him, and then like a lightbulb moment the answer came to him.

Matthews searched through the rest of the items on his desk, but what he was looking for was not there. He dashed from his office and to Mrs Lloyd-Hughes desk where the safe was placed behind her, squeezed past her empty seat and started to look through it. There in the back corner of the large safe was the shoebox filled with letters, the box he had taken from James Robinson's room. Inside there was letters from a number of people, but mostly from his father.

He carried the box back to his desk, ripped open one of Robinson's father's letters and held it up next to the damaged paper evidence. It was exactly as he suspected, the handwriting was the same, and even the paper and pen ink looked to be the same.

CHAPTER 22

Matthews left the office for home a litter after six thirty. Mrs Lloyd-Hughes had left over half an hour earlier. He locked all of the case items back into the safe before leaving and once outside was surprised to see Harvey waiting by the front entrance for him.

'Evening, sir.' He grinned upon seeing the detective.

'What on earth are you still doing here?'

'I usually stay late, sir. Evening feeding of the horses before putting them in for the night, then I'll be headed home.'

'Ah, I see. Well good night Harvey, I will see you in the morning.'

'By the way, sir,' he hollered after the detective. 'Gave Mrs Garner that letter this afternoon. She didn't seem too happy about it, especially when her husband came to the door and asked how she knew Mr Robinson. No matter though, she said she'd come to the station for nine tomorrow morning.' Matthews smirked, he was amused at just how much energy Harvey seemed to have at all times of the day.

'Thank you Harvey.' With that Matthews left the yard, and Harvey headed back to the stables. The walk home seemed longer this evening, and Matthews' feet felt heavier. He knew the work he had done so far had been positive, but the constant thought of his bag and notepad being stolen prayed on his mind.

Upon walking home he recognised a young man walking towards him, coming from the direction of the docks. It was David Turner, the man he had interviewed only last week from the Ocean Venture fishing fleet, a co-worker and friend of James Robinson. The thin man with short curly hair who wore filthy overalls smiled in recognition of the detective as they met in the street.

'Good evening detective.' Mr Turner acknowledge as they met. 'May I enquire how your enquiry is going?' His deep elegant voice did not match his appearance at all, and Matthews still found this amusing.

'Good evening Mr Turner,' Matthews had always been good at remembering people's names, especially when working. 'I am pleased to say I have been able to get some leads and have been working my way through them. Still a way to go though I'm afraid.'

'Well if there is anything I can do to help detective, you know where to find me.' He made to continue on his way, but the detective moved into his path to stop him.

'Can I ask you a quick question now?'

'Of course,' Turner replied.

'When I first spoke to you Mr Turner you mentioned that you had suspicions that Mr Robinson was looking for somebody here in Whitby.'

'Yes, sir. I recall him asking me if I knew somebody, can't remember the name now, but I overheard him asking people in the pub from time-to-time.'

'By any chance was the name Jackson?'

'Yes, that was it...somebody Jackson.' Turner beamed with delight at being able to confirm this information.

'Do you recall a first name?' Matthews quizzed, 'or if the name was male or female even?'

'Certainly a male, but I really couldn't be certain of the first name. As I told you before it was as though this person was a family member, he never seemed angry when mentioning the name, more concerned.'

'Thank you Mr Turner. Finally, before you go, do you know a Mrs Ellen Garner?'

'Oh her.' Turner rolled his eyes and scoffed. 'I'd forgotten about her. I know James was fucking her if that's what you mean. Don't know what he saw in her, she always seemed like a miserable old bitch if you ask me, not that I really saw her many times. Although I wouldn't be at all surprised if she was giving James money for his friendly visits, if you know what I mean.' He raised his eyebrows and gave the detective a knowing look. 'Wouldn't be the first time she's done it, with all that money and no husband around for the majority of the year.'

'I have a witness who claims to have seen Mr Robinson thrown out of the Black Horse Inn the night he died, before he headed in the opposite direction to his lodging, and in the direction of the bridge and the west cliff. I will be speaking to Mrs Garner to check if she knows anything and if Mr Robinson paid her a visit that night. I would ask that you let me know if you think of any more information Mr Turner.'

Matthews held out his hand and David Turner shook it. They parted ways and Matthews was suddenly feeling much more confident that the surname Jackson was linked to all this somehow. Now he just needed to figure out who that was.

As Matthews reached East Crescent he was surprised at how dark it was getting outside already. The street lamps were being lit on his street by a young boy carrying a ladder and a lit torch. Matthews wished he didn't have to go out this evening, he knew questioning Damian Campbell's so called security men was not going to be a fun task. He wished he could just stay home this evening, but he also knew that the sooner he cracked this case, the sooner he could leave Whitby.

Matthews was consumed within his own thoughts as he passed the young lamp lighter and turned up to the small stone steps leading to his front door. Upon reaching his door he almost dropped his keys in shock, and gasped with alarm at what lay up against his front door. It was his stolen briefcase.

CHAPTER 23

He grabbed the case in a dash and quickly unlocked his front door with shaking hands. Once inside he raced through to the kitchen to inspect the bag. There was nothing inside, his notepad had been taken. But clearly whoever had taken his bag knew where he lived, and for the first time in his professional career, Matthews felt vulnerable. Why would the person leave it on his doorstep? Was it to mock him, or was it a threatening gesture? Whatever the answer, Matthews suddenly felt sick to the pit of his stomach.

A number of hours later and Mathews was

preparing himself to go out for the evening. He knew the likelihood of speaking to Damian Campbell's men would be slim, especially with his plan of just hanging around Church Street, but he knew Mr Campbell would not permit him to speak with them formally. He had barely eaten anything due to his nauseous disposition, and right up to him heading for the door he was contemplating not going out that evening at all.

He left his house a little before 9pm. As he stepped out into the darkened street he felt wary, and found himself looking up and down the street in case anybody was around. He knew whoever had left his case on his doorstep was simply trying to get to him, and he was embarrassed to say it had worked. He locked his door in a hurry and marched on down the street towards the centre of town.

It was dark and the cloudy sky showed no signs of the moon or stars poking through. There was a casual breeze coming off the sea which cut through Matthews as he walked. Once he was out of sight of his house he lit up a cigarette and inhaled the smoke slowly, he was getting a headache. It was approximately a ten-minute walk to Church Street, and Matthews decided that the Black Horse Inn was probably his best spot to visit. It seemed far enough away from the Duke of York, the last thing he wanted was Damian Campbell catching him talking to his men; but it also had windows that he could survey the street in case his men were prowling.

The bar was much quieter than when he had called in on Saturday night, with only a handful of men around the bar. Matthews was greeted by the landlord Mr Henneberry who recognised him immediately.

'Evenin' detective. What can I get you this evening?' His gruff voice asked across the bar.

'Just a pint, thank you.'

'You 'ere asking more questions?' Mr Henneberry inquired whilst pulling him a pint of home brewed beer.

'Not this evening, you're safe.' He smirked as he handed over his money to the landlord. He took his drink and sat by the window alone, the perfect spot to look out for Mr Campbell's men.

Exhausted before he had even finished his first pint, Matthews contemplated going home once he had finished it. However, as he necked his final few dregs a friendly face walked into the pub. John Travers Cornwell, known simply by Jack, spotted his old school friend the moment he walked in.

'Benjamin,' he roared in his raucous voice. 'Back again so soon, people will start to talk.' He laughed a giggly kind of laugh. His thick dark unruly beard shook as he did so, and his usual tired pale face looked even more aged with his laughter. 'Let me buy you a drink, on me this time. You ran off before I could buy you another last time.'

'Okay, one drink,' Matthew replied, unable to hide his slight disappointment of not being able to leave. Jack went to the bar and returned minutes later carrying two identical pints of beer.

'So, you solved that case yet then?' Matthews couldn't hide his eye roll over his friends' comment. He explained his reason for being in the bar that evening to him and his positioning in the window. 'I did wonder,' Jack sniggered, 'thought you were selling yourself cheap.' He gave Matthews a shove as he laughed on. Matthews however was not laughing, and was instead looking out of the window. Just at that moment Damian Campbell's two security men had walked passed the window, and in the opposite direction to the Duke of York.

'Excuse me a moment.' He said to his friend in a hurry as he slid between Jack's chair and the next table, 'I'll be back in a minute,' and raced out of the door. The two men were walking at a fast pace and Matthews had to run to catch them up.

'Excuse me, gentleman. Could I speak with you a minute.'

'Piss off Mutton Shunter,' the largest of the men replied, and they both continued to walk towards the end of Church Street. Both men had dark balding hair, a dark greying beard, and wore all black. At a guess Matthews would have placed them both in their mid-forties. They clearly had no intention to stop, and so Matthews raced in front of them and stopped right in their track, causing them to halt. 'Did you not here me, piss off.'

'Gentlemen please, I implore you to give me just

two minutes of your time.' The two men were much larger than Matthews in both height and weight, and were certainly not intimidated by him.

'We are busy detective, not this evening thank you.' The larger one spoke again.

'How do you know I am a detective?'

'Everyone knows who you are, the chief's son who got the big promotion.' Matthews nostrils flared with annoyance at this remark, but thought better of arguing it. 'Plus, it was me who let you into the Duke to speak with DC.'

'Gentlemen, I am currently working on a murder investigation and so far I have statements claiming that you two were potentially the last people to see him alive. Now you can either give me two minutes now, or I can have you brought to the station for official questioning.' They looked at one and other as the detective spoke. 'I thought a more informal conversation would be more suited?' He was impressed by his own nerve, keeping his cool the entire time. The two men seemed hesitant to begin with, but with the threat of being called to the station they soon came around to reason.

'What do you want to know?'

'James Robinson was killed last Wednesday night. He was thrown out of the Black Horse Inn after a long drinking session for fighting, and I have witnesses telling me that you were around when he was outside the pub. Is this correct?'

'Sounds familiar,' said the larger man, the slightly shorter man had so far remained silent throughout.

'Witnesses tell me Mr Robinson was headed off down Church Street towards the direction of the bridge, and that you followed him.'

'Incorrect,' the large man interjected in a matter-of-fact tone.

'Then please tell me what really happened.'

'Yeah, we saw him outside the Black Horse Inn, but he was so pissed he wasn't worth it. He could barely walk he had drunk so much, and his speech was all over the place. Might have given him a kick as we passed, but he was so pissed I don't even know if he realised we were there to be honest.'

'So then what happened when you left him.'

'Nothing, as far as I could say. We were headed back to the Duke of York.'

'My eye witness tells me they say you follow Mr Robinson down Church Street in the opposite direction to the Duke.'

'Well we did go to the Duke, but about thirty minutes later we were walking past again and saw him still trying to walk away. We didn't touch him this time and walked straight passed him; think he was down passed the White Horse and Griffin pub by this time, so not made it very far. We were heading towards Grape Lane, cos you see that's where DC has a warehouse filled with beer kegs. We are usually back and forth bringing more down to the Duke. Not much cellar space there you see being on the corner and having Tate Hill beach behind.'

'So when you brought the kegs of beer back along Church Street did you see Mr Robinson again?'

'I saw him crossing the bridge,' the smaller of the

two men finally spoke, 'but I didn't think anything of it.'

'Do you know what time this would have been?'

'Think we got the kegs to the Duke for around midnight, so wouldn't have been much before then. Pub was filled and we were in the bar from midnight till closing, plenty of punters saw us there.' The larger man recalled. 'We done now?' he asked with impatience.

'Okay, thank you. I may need to speak with you again sometime though.'

'Whatever.' The larger man grunted, and they both charged off. Matthews returned to the Black Horse Inn where Jack was still sitting in the window with his pint.

'I thought you had done another runner on me.' He chuckled. 'Is my company really that bad?'

Matthews ended up staying at the pub for a number of rounds. His friend was enjoyable company and they laughed late into the night. It was after midnight when Matthews finally made it home, a little worse for wear; especially given he had not eaten very much before he had come out. With the knowledge that he had a meeting with Ellen Garner at nine o'clock the next morning, he knew he better get some rest. She was the last name on his list of people to speak with, and he knew that Mrs Garner's statement could be the final piece of the puzzle that helped him solve the case.

CHAPTER 24

Wednesday morning had arrived, and as Matthews lay in his bed a little worse for wear, he could not believe that he had been in Whitby almost a week already. Thankfully his old draughty house was much cleaner than when he had arrived, and with his sister bringing in second hand furniture and other useful items whilst he was out at work, the place was beginning to look homely. He knew his sister Charlotte would be disappointed to hear he was planning on returning to York, and it was for this reason why he had failed to tell her. He knew she would make a big scene, and make him feel bad about his decision; and he knew his father would be most appalled by the news too.

The sun peeking through his thin curtains meant it was going to be a beautiful day in the coastal town, and the sound of the seagulls outside from the crack of dawn meant that he had not really been asleep for the past hour at least. Instead he had been laying thinking about Grace, and wondering if she was okay. He knew he had no right, she had told him quite clearly that she wished to be left alone, yet he still could not get her from his mind.

Laid in his bed his stomach ached and his head pounded due to his alcohol consumption the previous night, and he wished he could just sleep in a little longer. It had been a long time since he had done a lot of drinking, and although he only consumed around six pints, for him that was a lot; especially on no food.

He finally pulled himself from his bed and proceeded on getting dressed. Harvey would be arriving soon to collect him, and no sooner had he thought it than there was a knock on the front door. Arriving home late he had not put out any fresh clothes ready, and so he raced from his bed naked, to his wardrobe to search for something to put on.

The ride to the station was quieter than usual, with Harvey realising the detectives delicate state. They pulled up outside at quarter to nine, and as Matthews headed to his office he noticed a woman sitting on a chair next to Mrs Lloyd-Hughes desk.

'D-Detective...' Mrs Lloyd-Hughes began.

'Just give me a minute,' he cut her off, 'then send her in.'

Matthews landed in his chair with a thud, he wished he had requested the meeting in the afternoon instead. With his notepad stolen he searched his desk for something else to write on, and quickly came across another notebook. He opened it out on his desk, checked his pencil worked by writing the date and Mrs Ellen Garner's name before shouting through to Mrs Lloyd-Hughes that he was ready. Seconds later the well-dressed woman in her early fifties walked into his office. She wore a long green dress, with matching hat, and pristine white gloves. She did not look at all pleased as she entered the detective's office.

'Good morning,' Matthews greeted, raising from his chair and stretching across his desk to shake the woman's hand. 'Mrs Garner I presume?' She took his hand to return the gesture but did not change her unimpressed expression. She removed her hat and placed it on one of the spare seats next to her, revealing her mousy hair that was tied up into a large bun. Her pale complexion and deep-set eyes made her look extremely angry. 'Please take a seat Mrs Garner, this won't take long.' She sat on the second wooden chair opposite Matthews, scowling at him.

'Can I ask why I have been summoned here? I'm sure you can understand the stress this is causing me being called to a police station.' Her plummy voice was exaggerated by her clear annoyance.

'Mrs Garner, my name is Detective Matthews and I have been given the case of James Robinson who was found dead on the beach last week. I believe you know this man?'

'Yes, but I don't know anything about his death.'

'I believe that, but what I am trying to do is get a

picture of Mr Robinson, so I can piece together any vital bits of information that may be key to discovering what happened to him.' Matthews was trying his hardest to stay alert, but was fighting back his heavy eyelids.

'What is it you need to know from *me*?' She said with such venom.

'On the night of Wednesday, May 6, Mr Robinson was spotted crossing the harbour bridge from the east cliff to the west cliff, and I wanted to know if he paid you a visit that night?'

'I don't know what you are trying to imply detective, but I can assure you he did not come to my house that evening.'

'I have statements from a number of people claiming that Mr Robinson was a frequent visitor to you Mrs Garner. Now I have no interest in this relationship…'

'There was no relationship,' she shouted.

'Very well, however as I was saying, I have no interest in *whatever* relationship you and Mr

Robinson had. However, what I do need to figure out is his movements that night which ultimately led to his death.' Mrs Garner opened her mouth as though ready to argue further but paused for a moment, her face like a bulldog with her lips pursed and brow wrinkled.

'I can assure you detective that Mr Robinson did not visit me that night. My husband had been home all of last week and I did not see anybody during that time other than him and my sister, who I met on the Tuesday.'

'When you and Mr Robinson did meet up, did he say much about himself on a personal level?'

'What do you mean?'

'Well did he tell you why he was in Whitby, for example? I know that he had not been here for more than a year, I wondered if he talked to you about anything like that?' Matthews was beginning to think that this interview was going nowhere.

'He came up from somewhere near Bristol, small village I think; I can't remember the name of it.' Her tone softened slightly, but her scowl remained. 'He was married, but didn't have many nice things to say about her.'

'Why was this?'

'She cheated on him, and went and got herself pregnant. They had been married for quite a long time and had been struggling to conceive for years. He had always blamed her, but then when he discovered she was pregnant to another man he went into a rage and left.'

'He told you all this?'

'He was more talkative after a few drinks, plus I don't think anybody else around here gave him the time of day to talk, not somebody who he trusted to keep his secrets anyway. I used to tell him things about myself, and I suppose after a while he felt comfortable to open up. I never asked him, mind you.'

'You just said the word "secrets", did Mr Robinson tell you secretive things?' Matthews sat up straight, his hangover slowly starting to fade, 'what secrets?'

'Just about his wife really. The man who got her pregnant was working for the council as a gardener in the village. She would talk to him most days, innocent at first, apparently, he wasn't much of a looker; and then one day she ended up taking him to their marital bed. Claimed to James it was only the one time, but of course that one time led to her getting pregnant didn't it. I don't think it was a long affair, most likely just the once. He was not a very bright young man, so James told me, and his wife clearly felt sorry for him.'

'Did Mr Robinson tell you why he'd come to Whitby?'

'Of course, apparently the gardener had been fired for sleeping with her, and through fear James was going to kill him he moved away; apparently he was a little weed of a man too so wouldn't have stood a chance against James. Anyway, James found out, and don't ask me by who because I don't know, but he found out that the man had moved up to Whitby.'

'Mrs Garner does the name Jackson mean anything to you?'

'Well yes, that is the name of the man James has been looking for. William Jackson.' Matthews gasped, finally he had a full name to go on.

'And did Mr Robinson tell you about his search for Mr Jackson often?'

'Not often, but he mentioned it once or twice. The last time I saw him was probably a week before he died, he was deflated at being here so long without finding the man and was talking about returning south. With my husband due to be home for a week I didn't think I would see James again, presumed he would have gone home in that time.'

'Do you know of anybody who would want to harm Mr Robinson?'

'I have to confess detective that I do not know any of James' contacts or acquaintance in Whitby. We certainly do not go out in public together. I know he was taking opium and the rumour is that whoever he owed money to finally got their payback on him, but that of course is idol gossip.'

'Mrs Garner do you know if Mr Robinson had any other friends, or relations with anybody, on the west cliff side of town? I ask because he was seen headed over to this side of town the night he died and I am trying to figure out where he could have been going.'

'Not that I know. I know he lived on Church Street, a guesthouse I believe. He worked on one of the fishing docks on this side of the river, but again I could not say which one. Other than the name he was searching for, and a little about his family down south I can't say I knew him all that well.'

Matthews wrote up Ellen Garners notes in front of her and checked through the details with her to confirm. He was now more confident than ever about the case, and felt he was closer than ever to cracking it. Mrs Garner claimed that William Jackson was a scrawny little man, so if James had found him then surely a man of his build would not struggle to defend himself against such a small man. With that in mind Matthews showed Mrs Garner to the door and thanked her for calling in. He had now gone through his list of names he wished to talk to, and the events of James Robinson's final night were finally starting to fall into place.

CHAPTER 25

There was a loud knock on the office door causing Matthews to jump, and without invitation in walked his father.

'Good news my son,' he declared in his roaring voice, 'Bristol police have been able to locate Mr Robinson's wife and have informed her of his death.' He took the seat opposite Matthews and beamed with delight at the news he brought. 'So once the investigation is done, we can have him sent down to his family. Is everything okay?'

'Just tired I guess,' he wasn't totally lying, but he was certainly not going to admit to being hung over either, 'and I need to finish writing up my notes that co-inside with Mrs Garner's statement and continue with the timeline of Mr Robinson's final movements. Then I need to start looking into a William Jackson.' He would normally end up in an argument with his father when they spoke, but his exhaustion meant he could barely be bothered to even talk to him.

'Plenty still to do then I see, keep up the good work.' He stood to leave again but instead of walking toward the door he moved towards the window. 'Young Harvey doing okay?' He could see him from the window grooming one of the horses.

'He is certainly enthusiastic; I will give him that,' replied Matthews, leaning on his desk with no energy to also look out of the window. 'Couple of years I don't see any reason he couldn't start his training.' Matthews began rubbing his forehead as he spoke, enjoying the darkness his hands caused over his eyes. 'Why do you care about him anyway?'

'Oh no reason really,' the chief commented, moving away from the window, 'but it does look good to grow our own, not always easy to get officers to move to Whitby, being a small town and all. By the way your sister is making fish tonight, and you know she is just like your mother and makes too much, so please do come around for your dinner.'

'Sure.' Was all the reply he could manage. Normally he'd say no but knew it would lead into his father talking more into encouraging him, this way he might go away sooner. His father had clearly thought this too and looked startled by his sons answer, he was almost speechless.

'Right...well, I will see you this evening then.' His father said and swiftly left the office.

By four o'clock Matthews had still barely done his paperwork and decided it was time for him to go home. He knew if he left now he'd be able to take a nap before heading to his father and sisters house for dinner. He put away his paperwork, wished Mrs Lloyd-Hughes a good night and left the station. He had with him his briefcase with a new notebook inside and felt himself embarrassed with it after what had happened only the previous day. Could the person who stole it be watching him?

***

Harvey, who had been following Grace most of the afternoon, was preparing himself to head back to the station to feed the horses. He had followed her as she picked up groceries and she had been on her own for the entire afternoon.

Grace turned up onto Flowergate, and Harvey knew that this was a short cut in the direction of her house. As Harvey turned to head back to the station he saw approaching him from the other direction Grace's fiancé. Harvey's heart stopped for a moment as he thought the man was headed straight for him, but he simply brushed past Harvey without even a glance and marched on over to Grace.

'What the fuck have you been buying now, do we really need all this shit.'

'It's just something for dinner tonight, and I was thinking I could make a dessert with these ingredients.' He leaned in and kissed her on the cheek, but she pulled back as though appalled. 'Have you been drinking again?'

'So what if I have, who the fuck do you think you

are, my mother?'

'No, but aren't you supposed to be at work?'

He did not reply, and simply slapped her hard across the face. The sound of his palm slapping against her cheek could be heard over the noise of the horse and carriages that passed on by. Graces gasped in shocked clutching her shopping raised a hand to hold her face.

Harvey wasted no time at all and turned and ran for the direction of the station. He knew that Matthews would want to know about this immediately. He only got two streets away when he saw the detective walking home in his direction.

'Sir…' he panted, 'come, quick. Grace.'

Matthews eyes widened and he immediately began to run to catch up with Harvey and follow him up and around onto Flowergate where the fiancé could now be heard shouting even before Matthews could see him.

'What have I told you about doing that in public,' her fiancé yelled at her.

'I'm sorry, I was just trying to…'

'Well don't bother.' He threw something at her, it was one of the shopping bags that had originally been held by Grace, it was in a brown paper bag and looked solid. It hit her square in the face before landing on the floor next to the road, and she started to cry as she retrieved the item from the floor. 'Hurry up, for fuck's sake.' But this only made Grace more upset, she could not move from where she stood and instead began to flood with tears. Her fiancé was already walking off ahead, and hearing her cry turned and shouted at her again. 'Are you coming?' Grace continued to sob as she clutched the item in the brown paper bag to her chest.

Matthews stopped upon seeing them both, he hesitated as whether to intervene, he knew Grace would not approve, but it distressed him to see her like this. There were people walking up and down the street, but none of them got involved. Finally, her fiancé let out a loud groan and started walking back to Grace, dragging his feet as though fed up of walking, and without warning he lifted up his arm and smacked Grace across the face, this time much harder than the last one. She let out a toe-curling scream, dropped her parcel and fell to the floor. Matthews wasted no time at all and raced to her side. He put himself between Grace and her fiancé just in time as he was clearly going to hit her again. Matthews grab the man by the arm.

'What the fuck?' he shouted, pushing Matthews off of him. 'Piss off, this has nothing to do with you.'

'Leave her alone now.' Matthews had never felt so angry, his entire body was shaking.

'Or what?' The man got right up into the detective's face, his warm breath smelt terrible of tobacco and alcohol. Grace watched as the two men squared up against one and other, tears still falling down her face and her breathing heavy as she tried to desperately control her sobbing.

'Grace will be coming with me now, you have done enough damage here.' Matthews tried to say it as calmly as he possibly could but felt his lips trembling with rage.

'Like hell you are.'

The man punched the detective in the stomach. Matthews gasped in shock, he had been winded but managed to retaliate and pushed the man backwards into the street. This only angered the fiancé even further and he began a full-blown attack on the detective.

Both men were now throwing punches at one and other, with Matthews receiving several blows to the head and torso. The other man also got his fair share of hits too as Matthews landed blows to his upper body. The scuffle had now attracted a small crowd, some of which looked shocked, others cheering on the fight as though it was entertainment. The man kicked Matthews in the shin, followed by another blow to the face. Matthews could feel that he had blood on his face but was not sure where it was coming from. Matthews managed to hold his own, and threw several punches back at the man. Within a minute of the fight breaking out a police officer rushed in to break up the fight. Thankfully the officer recognised Matthews immediately and instinctively restrained the other man, who tried to then fight the officer. With another officer not far behind the two of them managed to restrain the fiancé and arrest him for causing a disturbance.

Matthews was exhausted and returned to Grace's side, she was still sitting on the floor. She was holding her head that was bleeding after the impact on the ground, and her now fading black eye that Matthews had seen last week looked as though it might return. He took out a handkerchief from his pocket and placed it on the side of Grace's head where the blood was coming from. She tensed at the pain from the pressure but did not stop him.

'You should have used that on your face, it's covered in blood,' she whispered, still slightly out of breath from crying. He kept his handkerchief on her head, and wiped his face on his long sleeved shirt. More blood wiped onto it than he had anticipated as both his nose and lip was bleeding.

With one hand holding his handkerchief onto the side of her head, his other hand casually found her hand, and he held it for a moment quite naturally. She seemed to breathe a sigh of relieve as she let the detective hold her, leaning into him her tear stained face caused his shirt and waistcoat to become damp.

Matthews too felt a little sore from the fight, with his ribs and stomach throbbing and his face feeling like such a mess. This certainly had not helped his hangover.

'Can I help you home?' Matthews spoke softly to her after what had felt like a long time sitting on the floor. He helped her to her feet and she stood with a wobble before managing to find her balance. Her head was no longer bleeding, although her hair was now matted and covered in dried blood.

'Thank you, that would be much appreciated,' she whispered back to him. He took her by the arm and helped her back along the street.

They didn't speak the entire way back to Grace's house, and Matthews let her direct him. She lived in a rather grand mid terrace house and once through the door Grace felt she had enough energy to see herself through to the kitchen. Matthews was a little hesitant as to whether he should follow her inside, or if he should let himself out. He decided to follow, and once in the long alley kitchen instructed her to take a seat.

'That was a nasty bump on the head, you need to take it easy for a little bit. Let me help you clean up the blood before I go.'

'Honestly detective you have done more than enough to help, I thank you, but I think I will be okay from here. Plus, I think it may be you that needs more of a clean-up than me.' She gave a little snigger at the sight of him, his hair was a mess and there was dried blood over his face, hands and arms.

'I am not leaving you until I know you are okay, now sit down please and I will fill a bowl with warm water to clean you up.'

Grace instructed Matthews from her seat where to find a bowl and cloth to use for cleaning her head. He boiled a kettle of water on the hob and as they waited for it to heat up Matthews tried to think of something to say other than the obvious. He had already told her before to file a report against her husband-to-be; she already knew his opinion on that front.

'Do you have any food in the house, can I get you anything in?'

'I do, thank you, I went to the market this morning and have vegetables in the pan over there ready to cook.' Her voice was starting to sound like its old self again, and the colour was starting to return to her cheeks.

Once the water had heated Matthews poured it into a bowl and soaked a small cloth in it for a number of seconds before squeezing out the excess water, and gently pressing it against her head wound. She flinched at the pain and took in a breath through gritted teeth.

'I'm sorry.' Matthews hesitated.

'It's okay,' she replied with her eyes downcast. She was fiddling with her fingernails.

Once her head was fully cleaned Matthews emptied and refilled the bowl of water to try and clean up his own face and hands. With no mirror in the kitchen he struggled, and so Grace took the cloth from him and took over wiping away the blood stains from his face; being as gentle as possible. Her washing his face so gently felt almost intimate between them both, yet neither seemed to mind and Matthews secretly enjoyed it.

Once they were both cleaned Matthews made them both a drink and stayed with her for a while longer until he knew she was certainly going to be okay.

'What will happen to him?' she wondered, sipping her tea.

'He will be held overnight more than likely, to calm down. He will more than likely be charged for attacking an officer, but depending on whether or not they see him as a threat he could be out later in the day. Unless…' He stopped himself from saying 'somebody makes a statement' but it was too late, she looked at him as though she knew exactly what he was getting at. He changed the subject quickly, and began talking about himself instead, telling her about his job and why he was on the train that day they first met. Talking with Grace felt effortless to Matthews, he had never felt this comfortable simply making small talk with somebody before; and his hangover felt less imposing since his fight.

Time flew by, and Matthews finally left at seven,

he was late for his sister's meal and he knew she would be angry with him. Grace walked him to the door.

'Are you sure you are going to be okay?' he asked for the millionth time as they stood in the doorway.

'Yes, thank you detective for your help, I appreciate your kindness.' Matthews took her hand, he had intended to shake it goodbye, but instead it turned into an awkward hand holding moment that both of them let go of without acknowledging.

'And you're sure you don't need me to get you anything, food, drinks, anything at all?'

'Good night detective. Thank you again.' She gave him a warm smile and closed the door. Matthews immediately regretted not begging her to testify against her fiancé for his clear domestic abuse towards her, and even wondered whether knocking on her door again to do so would be out of order. He decided against it, she had been through enough today already and he didn't want to stress her out any further. He knew he needed to take a step back from her situation, but this was a struggle when he knew deep down that he had feelings for her. But how could he think like that when she was planning to get married in just a couple of months' time, and he was planning to leave for York again once this case was over.

CHAPTER 26

Matthews barely slept a wink; he couldn't stop thinking about Grace. When morning finally arrived and he was getting ready to leave for the office, he debated whether or not to pay her a visit on route. He must have changed his mind so many times between getting out of bed and leaving the house, but once out of the door he finally decided to leave her in peace. After all she was engaged, and he couldn't force her to testify. Thankfully he had escaped a black eye from his fight, but he was still sore and had a cut lip.

'Morning, sir,' Harvey greeted him as usual,

though this time with a large blanket over his head to protect him from the heavy downpour of rain that seemed to be set in for the day. The horses and carriage were parked outside his house ready to go, and Matthews dashed through the rain into the back of the carriage as quickly as he could, handing Harvey an umbrella to use whilst driving the horses. 'Thank you,' he beamed, 'straight to the station is it?'

'Yes please Harvey, and do come up to my office with me too, I want to show you all the evidence we have collected so far, I think you will be quite surprised what we have.'

'Really, sir?' Harvey's eyes lit up with delight.

'Well I'm sure I remember you mentioning wanting to be a police officer one day, best way to start is to go through the evidence.' Matthews felt a little burst of joy knowing he had made the lads morning with such a small gesture. The ride to the station was damp, as the rain continued to hammer down; causing the sloping street to look like a river.

Harvey guided the horses as close to the station

door as possible so the detective could jump out and in without getting soaked, and using the umbrella Harvey managed to stay reasonably dry too as he took the horses back to the stables. As Matthews approached his office, he was surprised not to hear the sound of Mrs Lloyd-Hughes tapping away at her typewriter, and when he saw her desk was empty he wondered where on earth she could be. His own office door was slightly ajar and when he swung it open he found Mrs Lloyd-Hughes sitting on the sofa in there, with Grace.

'I'm sorry, s-sir, but you see this seemed a more comfortable place for Miss Clayson.' He had already spotted that Grace had been crying, and Mrs Lloyd-Hughes was holding a box of tissues for her.

'That is quite alright,' he replied with hesitation, 'would you like me to leave and give you ladies some space?'

'No...' sniffled Grace, 'I came to see you detective.' Matthews took a seat behind his desk and waited apprehensively. Mrs Lloyd-Hughes stood, placed the box of tissues on the sofa next to Grace and excused herself, closing the door firmly on her way out.

'So…' Matthews dithered, 'how are you feeling this morning?'

'Surprisingly I slept quite well, and my head is less sore this morning.' It was clear by her body language that she too was feeling a little awkward. 'I want to thank you for what you did yesterday. So many people would have just walked passed and left me.'

'Oh I don't think they would, you'll be surprised just how many people step in when they think somebody is being wrongly…' He paused, not wanting to use the word attacked yet his mind had frozen as it frantically tried to think of another word.

'Well it was very kind of you,' Grace said.

'You did not need to come all the way to the station just to thank me.'

'No, but I wanted to. I also…,' she took a whimpered breath as she suppressed her tears, 'I know you have been wanting me to come and report him for some time now, but I have been too frightened, he will not be happy and if he finds out I can only imagine the rage he will go into.'

'We will keep you safe, I promise. He is due to be released shortly but if you really are here to testify against him for domestic abuse then I can send word not to release him yet. Would you like me to do that?' Grace nodded, but could not bring herself to say anything out loud.

Matthews raised from his chair and made for the door, speaking in a hushed voice to Mrs Lloyd-Hughes outside so that Grace could not make out their conversation, before returning to the office and sitting beside her on the sofa.

'Tell me everything, from the beginning. How did you meet him?' He wanted nothing more than to place his hand on hers that were tightly squeezed together on her lap anxiously. 'Take your time.'

'He comes from a wealthy family,' she begun, looking down at her hands the entire time that she spoke. 'My parents had been friends with his and had decided when we were children that we would be matched. Both our parents live in Pickering, so not far at all. In his late teens, he joined the army, and so I didn't see him very much at all for a number of years. I am five years younger than him, so it was not ideal to marry before he left. When he left the army last year, he was offered a job in Whitby, which he took immediately and I was expected to marry him as soon as possible. I managed to convince my parents to give us some time to reacquaint ourselves, you know, before having a ceremony. I agreed to move to Whitby with him, we have only been here six months, and our wedding is planned for August.' She paused for a moment, and Matthews was shocked by how open she had suddenly become.

'So how long after moving to Whitby with him did he change, when did he start becoming violent?' He cringed at using the word violent. Normally he had no issues questioning witnesses, and in York this was his usual type of interview, but with Grace it felt different and he did not want to upset her in anyway.

'Straight away.' She let out a long deep breath.

'His new job was desk based and he felt trapped. Whitby felt too quiet for him, and because I...' She looked up from her hands and met the detectives eye for the first time, a discomfort in what she wanted to say came over her. 'I refused to...you know, before marriage, he got angry and took every little annoyance out on me.' Her face flushed pink with embarrassment.

'There is nothing to be embarrassed about,' Matthews placed his hand onto hers, he knew it was unorthodox in a witness interview but he could not stop himself. Grace did not seem to mind and even turned her hand over so she could hold his.

Grace ended up staying in Matthews office for a number of hours that morning. After having their initial chat Matthews then began to write up her statement detailing all the times he had hurt her. Just before midday Mrs Lloyd-Hughes brought a tray with a pot of tea for them both, and once they had finished compiling her statement, he got her to sign it.

'Will he be released today?' Grace enquired as she made to leave the office shortly after midday.

'There is a chance he could be; however, I will send this statement through to the correct department as soon as possible and stress to them that his release will only put you in threat if he decided to let off steam. I will keep you updated.'

'I don't have anywhere else to go, the house is his so I will need to go back to Pickering and stay with my parents. I'd have to arrange a carriage.'

'I can arrange for you to stay somewhere for a short period, somewhere he wouldn't know to look for you.' He didn't really want her to move away, but he knew he couldn't offer her a room at his house too, not only was it completely unprofessional but also a little forward. He quickly racked his brain to think of a solution. 'My sister.' He blurted out, not fully thinking. 'My sister has a spare room; you can stay there for a little time if you wanted?'

'Are you sure she wouldn't mind?' She looked slightly baffled by this gesture.

'Of course not. If you pack a bag up this afternoon, we can take you around later today. I can collect you in the carriage, or you can come back to the station; whichever.' He knew what he was promising was not exactly common practise for the police department, and his father, the chief of police, would be furious at him for doing this. However, he did not care at that moment in time, he had strong feelings for Grace and wanted to know she was safe.

Shortly afterwards Grace bid goodbye to Matthews, and thanked Mrs Lloyd-Hughes on her way past. Matthews watched as she walked along the corridor and out of sight whilst he handed the statement to his secretary. He was about to turn back to his office when somebody coughed in a way to be noticed. It was Harvey, and he was sitting on a chair in the outer office waiting for the detective.

'Harvey, yes, sorry. Come on through, we were going to go through the evidence weren't we.' He had completely forgotten about Harvey, and felt dreadful for making him wait so long. 'Let's see if we can pick up any missing pieces that can help us crack this case.'

CHAPTER 27

Matthews and Harvey laid out all of the evidence for the case across his desk. Harvey was surprised just how much paperwork the detective had written up as well as the number of different items they had.

'So you will remember this,' Matthews pointed to the sea water damaged pieces of paper, 'this was our first pieces of evidence that was discovered in Mr Robinson's pocket.'

'I do,' replied Harvey with excitement, 'and we discovered that one of them had a stamp on of the fish fleet that he worked for.'

'Exactly. Now if you look at the other one with Havelock Place written on, you will see…' he leaned over and pulled forward the shoebox of letters he had taken from James Robinson's room, 'that the handwriting is exactly the same as these letters from his father.' Harvey held up the tatty piece of paper next to one of the letters to compare.

'Oh yes, I see that. But what does that mean?'

'It means that his father was potentially helping his son locate the man he was looking for. Why would he carry a letter in his pocket when he had them all stored in this box? It's because it contained some information that he intended to act upon.'

'But the officers questioned people on Havelock Place, sir. Surely they would have picked something up?'

'Whoever did it is not planning on coming forward to confess. Now we of course know that Johnny King lives just off of Havelock Place and Mr Robinson owes him money, but there is nothing to indicate that Mr King has any connections to the man Mr Robinson was in search of.'

'Do you still think Mr King is a potential suspect?' Harvey was starting to look puzzled.

'Yes, and I have put in a request to formally speak with him. He of course lives on the West Coast, and Robinson was seen heading towards the West Coast, so Mr King is not off of the hook just yet.' He shuffled through the paperwork and handed Harvey another one to read, 'Mrs Garner mentioned that the man Mr Robinson was searching for was a tiny little fellow who stood no chance against Robinson, so although I want to find out who this man, was I am still not overly convinced this so called tiny man could bring down a tall well build man like Mr Robinson alone.'

'But what about the coroner report?' Harvey pulled it closer, 'It says he had an undissolved pill found in him, guessed to be codeine but not confirmed, in him?'

'That is true, and I have already asked Mrs Lloyd-Hughes to get a list together for me of all the stores in town that sell it, as well as asking them to check their records for anything else Mr Robinson may have purchased. We should then be able to see if Mr

Robinson purchased this himself. It is quite a common over the counter drug though, so even if he didn't purchase it himself it could still prove difficult to pin point who did.' Matthews flicked through more of his notes, showing Harvey what they said.

'So what about Damian Campbell and his security men,' asked Harvey, 'are they no longer on the suspect list?'

'I will certainly be keeping an eye on them, that is for sure.'

As Matthews then re-read the statement from Ellen Garner out loud to Harvey a sudden realisation hit him. He stopped reading aloud, his mind suddenly racing as he tried to piece things together in his head. He thought he might have just realised something, but it all seemed blurred in his mind.

'Is everything okay detective?' Harvey was concerned. Matthews did not immediately reply and closed his eyes as he tried to put together his new thoughts. They were like a fuzzy puzzle in his mind that was trying to show him something but he was struggling to figure out why they fit. Harvey sat in silence waiting, and finally the detective spoke.

'It has been staring us in the face this whole time.' He opened his eyes with a start. 'Harvey go and get the horses ready, we need to make a trip out right now.' His wide eyes continued to look into space as he went over and over in his head what he was still piecing together.

'Detective?' Harvey stood to leave, but was more confused than ever as to what was happening.

'Harvey lets go, now,' Matthews blinked and almost jumped out of his own train of thought, 'we need to go now, I will meet you out front in ten minutes. I just need to put all of this away first. Harvey dashed out of the office.

Matthews tidied away the items on his desk as quickly as he could, almost dropping them as he ran over and over in his mind what he was thinking. Questioning himself and re-going over his thoughts. He was also in a hurry as he wanted to get this visit over with as soon as possible so he could then go and help Grace move her belongings to his sisters. He raced down the stairs of the station, almost landing at the bottom with a thud, and dashed out of the front door just in time to see Harvey guiding the large black horses around.

'Where too. Sir?' Harvey asked, huddled under the detective's umbrella.

'Aim for Havelock Place, but park on the end of John Street, just like we did when we went to see Johnny King.' He jumped into the carriage and they were soon off through the dense rain. Harvey wondered why the detective was so keen to go back and see Johnny King, surely he wasn't going to get any further with him, was he?

Matthews felt twitchy in the back of the carriage, and the cold weather did little to help. He knew that if his hunch was correct then he may have found the final piece of the puzzle that could solve the entire case.

CHAPTER 28

The rain was starting to slow when they reached the corner of John Street, and Harvey tied up the horses as the detective emerged from the carriage. He spotted two officers walking towards them, and stopped them for a moment.

'Good afternoon officers, I am Detective Matthews…'

'We know who you are detective,' the taller thinner of the officers replied, 'how can we be of service?'

'Would I be correct in thinking that you two

gentlemen were the ones who did door-to-door enquiries of the residents in Havelock Place?' He recognised the younger one coming to his house to inform him that somebody had admitted to building the penny hedge.

'That would be us, sir.' He grinned as though proud of himself.

'Well gentleman the investigation has brought me back to this street, I may require we speak with all the residents again. However, before we do so there is one house that is at the top of my list which I am headed for right now.'

A front door slammed shut along Havelock Place, and Matthews, Harvey and the two officers instinctively looked to see who it was. It was Ernest O'Sullivan, the dog walker who had found the body only a week ago. He spotted the detective and officers immediately and gave them a questioning stare before walking off in the opposite direction with his little King Charles spaniel in tow.

'Thank you for your time men, I will keep you updated on any further enquiries.' Matthews then took off at speed down Havelock Place, Harvey racing to keep up with him. Ernest O'Sullivan was now out of sight, but to Harvey's surprise that was not the house Matthews aimed for.

Matthews knocked on the door of number five Havelock Place, and after a couple of minutes standing in the now lighter rain, Mrs Hutton answered the door. The elderly woman looked surprised to see the detective on her doorstep.

'Can I help you detective?' Her soft voice was almost lost in the sound of the wind and rain, and her small frame made her look fragile in the large doorway. Her pale complexion and white hair a huge contrast to the black floor-length dress she always wore.

'Could I come in please Mrs Hutton, I need a word.'

She invited Matthews and Harvey inside and directed them both through to the kitchen this time at the back of the house. As they entered the kitchen Matthews was surprised to see just how disorganised it was. All of the counters, and even the kitchen table was littered with books, paperwork and a layer of dust; a huge contrast compared to the sitting room Matthews had sat in on his last visit.

'Do excuse the mess detective,' Mrs Hutton commented as she gestured him towards one of the dining chairs, 'the house work does get on top of me sometimes.' Matthews took the chair out of politeness, but Harvey decided to stand. Matthews found his eyes wondering around the room, he had never seen so much clutter in one room before. 'Can I make you a drink detective?'

'No, I think we won't be staying for very long, I was actually calling around to ask if...' he abruptly stopped what he was saying as something had caught his attention. In the corner of the kitchen was a wall mounted shelf, filled with old jars that looked as though they and their contents had not been used for years. The shelves were also quite high and there was no way that Mrs Hutton could reach the higher shelves alone.

Matthews raised from this seat and walked over to the shelves, Mrs Hutton watched on puzzled, as did Harvey.

'Mrs Hutton do you mind if I look at something on this shelf?'

'Not at all detective.' Her brow creased as she leaned to see around Matthews at what he found so interesting. He reached up to the top shelf where poking behind one of the dirty jars was a journal like book, a notebook. Matthews lifted it down and instantly recognised it as his own.

'Mrs Hutton I was wondering if your nephew was home, and if I could speak with him?'

'Willy? Well yes he is upstairs.' She was looking more and more confused.

'Mrs Hutton is your nephew's full name, William Jackson?' Mrs Hutton let out a small gasp of shock and before she could answer the detective Willy appeared in the doorway, his eyes wide as he saw the detective holding onto the notebook.

'Mr Jackson, could I have a word please…'

Willy Jackson bolted from the room and made a dash for the front door. Matthews immediately pursued with Harvey following closely behind. Willy

Jackson threw open the door, jumped down the stone steps that led down to the pavement and raced down the street as quickly as he could. Unfortunately for him though Matthews was much faster and caught him up only a couple of metres away from his front door. He grabbed Willy Jackson by the arm and spun him around. Jackson launched an immediate attack and punched the detective square in the face causing Matthews to momentarily halt by the sheer surprise of the force. He was also in incredible pain still from his fight yesterday. Jackson raced on again and Harvey, who had now caught up, went also to grab Jackson by the arm but was immediately shoved back with such strength that it caused him to stumble backward, leading him to trip down the curb and land in the road with a thud.

'Stop,' shouted Matthews, who again went to grab the man and instead found himself tackling Jackson to the ground where he managed to restrain his arms behind him.

'Get off of me.' He screamed, and tried to spit in the detectives face. Jackson was desperate not to give in and was kicking and thrashing his entire body around trying to escape his restraint. 'Who the fuck do you think you are? I haven't done anything wrong.'

'Harvey bring the carriage over.' Matthews shouted. Harvey wasted no time in running over to the carriage which was still parked in view at the end of John Street, and pulled the horses around.

'I said get the fuck off me.' Jackson continued to jerk his body on the ground, causing his entire body to smack against the paving stones. Matthews tried to hold him down harder in the hope to minimise the damage Jackson was causing to himself.

'Tell me why you have my notebook in your kitchen William?'

Matthews knew this was not the time to question him, but he hoped Jackson talking might stop his violent thrashing. He did not answer him and continued to shout and scream, and the screams were now sounding as though he was in pain. Residents of the street were starting to appear in doorways, and passers-by stopped to see what was going on.

'Let me go…I have done nothing wrong.' Both Jackson and Matthews were exhausted trying to battle one and other on the floor, what was taking Harvey so long with the carriage?

'Mr Jackson if you have done nothing wrong then why run?'

Jackson went rigid with exhaustion. His heavy breathing the only indication he was okay. Matthews dare not release his grip by even an inch, and quickly looked up to see Harvey guiding the horses over. They were all soaked in the sodden ground and light rain.

'Mr Jackson I am arresting you under the suspicion of murdering Mr James Robinson.' Mrs Hutton was now standing in her doorway watching, the horror on her face at what was unfolding before her. 'We will be taking you to the station immediately for questioning.' Matthews and Harvey managed to get Mr Jackson into the carriage, although they almost had to carry him between them due to his own attempts to stop them.

Matthews had to continuously restrain Jackson in the carriage, as he persisted on attacking him and trying to escape. He even tried biting Matthews in a bid to be let go, but despite all of his attempts and attacks on the detective, he did not manage to escape the carriage and was brought to the station where he was left in a cell overnight to calm before questioning the next day.

EPILOGUE

As usual Matthews was running late to one of his families evening meals. He wouldn't normally be so keen to attend, it wasn't a special occasion or anything, but he was most eager to attend this evening as Grace was now living there for a short time. She had moved into the spare bedroom on Thursday night, and was already getting along with Matthews younger sister Charlotte as though they had been old friends.

When Matthews finally arrived, he was greeted by Charlotte and Grace who were busy setting the table. Grace beamed with delight the moment Matthews walked into the dining room, and

Matthews could not hide the flush of pink that glowed his cheeks.

His father was in the sitting room enjoying a glass of wine, which was supposed to be for the dinner table. He was joined by John Nicholson, Charlottes fiancé.

'Ah there you are my son.' His father quickly bolted over to greet him the moment he walked through the door. His voice was so loud that the entire household heard him. 'I have not had time to read your report yet, but congratulations on closing the case. How on Earth did you do it so quickly, I expected you to be on that case another week at least.' He leaned in closer to whisper in his son's ear, 'and I would rather you talk to me about that than have to keep listening to John going on and on about football.' He placed his arm around his sons shoulder and led him through to the dining table that was beautifully set out for dinner. Matthews parents' house was not small, and was tastefully decorated throughout with lavish paintings, plants and expensive furniture.

'Pops, William Jackson made a full confession

yesterday after we presented him with all the details we had on the case. It wasn't actually enough to convict him, or fully prove him to be the murderer; it simply pointed to him being the man Robinson was looking for. But he clearly didn't know that and told us everything.'

hey sat down at the table and Charlottes fiancé John came and joined them.

'How on Earth did you know to go and see him then?'

'When I was going through all the evidence and notes with Harvey it hit me. Mrs Hutton had mentioned that her nephew had been with her less than a year, and we know that Mr Robinson was here a similar time looking for somebody. Jackson never left the house because he was worried that Robinson would find him, so this is why it took Robinson so long looking for him. The description Mrs Garner gave of the young man just seemed too familiar and it hit me that Mrs Hutton's nephew fit it. I of course couldn't be certain but I knew it was worth checking out.'

'Okay, but how does this actually tie in with Jackson killing Robinson?'

'Robinson had received a letter from his father the night before his death with the address of Mrs Hutton, he had done some digging and discovered where Jackson had gone. Robinson didn't want to do anything during the day as there would be people around, so planned to go late at night. Unfortunately for him though he got a little too drunk at the pub and arrived on Mrs Hutton's doorstep in such a state he was unable to beat Jackson as he planned. I believe he was not planning a simple punch up, and Jackson was probably the planned dead body.'

'I still don't understand how Jackson pulled off killing him though?' The chief confessed.

'Jackson heard Robinson banging on the door and came rushing downstairs before Mrs Hutton, who slept at the back of the house, heard anything. He confessed yesterday that he stole some of Mrs Hutton's pills, that she just leaves casually next to her arm chair, and forced them down Robinsons throat. Jackson tells us that Robinson was already nearly unconscious due to the alcohol so had no trouble getting the pills down him.'

'So how on Earth did they end up on the beach?' The chief scratched his head. 'I saw Jackson and he is a tiny fellow.'

'Jackson managed to get Robinson on his feet and walked him to the beach. He thought that by tying him to the penny hedge it would keep him anchored down enough for him to drown, the penny hedge would break and float away and that Robinson would just be presumed a drowning victim. But you see he tied the penny hedge a little too tight to Robinson's wrists and it didn't wash away.'

'As much as I am not doubting you son, how exactly did Jackson think this was going to work, and didn't he know the overdose would have done it?'

'William Jackson's auntie told me that his mental condition puts him to the mental age of twelve years old. Although he is in his early twenties and managed to get Robinson's wife pregnant, I don't think he is fully aware of what he had really done.

Even questioning him yesterday I don't fully believe he has understood the seriousness of everything. I truly believe he thought this plan would be perfect and untraceable back to him.'

'Dinner is served,' Charlotte interrupted, walking in with a large plate of cooked meats. Grace followed behind with a tray of smaller bowls and plates filled with potatoes and vegetables. 'No more work talk this evening.' His sister chuckled as she lay down the food.

'This looks delightful Lotty.' Matthews complemented his sister who took the chair opposite him, next to her fiancé. His father had the chair at the head of the table and this left Grace taking the seat next to Matthews.

'Thank you again for letting me stay.' Grace gestured towards Matthews father. His father looked at his son with disapproving eyes. He didn't dislike Grace, just his son's unconventional assistance to her.

'Have you decided if you will be staying in Whitby?' Matthews enquired as plates were passed around the table.

'I'm not sure right now, I have nowhere really to live and can't take your fathers hospitality for too much longer.' She smiled at the chief of police.

'I do hope you will stay in Whitby,' Matthews blurted out, his eyes suddenly widened at the realisation of what he had just said. She smiled and squeezed her hand on his under the table.

If you enjoyed this Detective Matthews novel please do consider leaving a small review on Amazon or Goodreads.

Thank you

The Penny Hedge

I have always found legends and old wives tales fascinating and when I had decided I was going to write Detective Matthews own book I first turned to local stories for a little inspiration.

I came across the Penny Hedge ceremony which I found fascinating, I included its origin story within this book. Over the course of many months I then worked out a murder mystery story that would allow me to include the origin story as well as having the penny hedge play a vital role in the plot.

Planting Penny Hedge, Whitby

Behind The Scenes

In 2015 I released D: Whitby's Darkest Secret, and it was from this book that the character Detective Matthews began to intrigue me.

I have always loved the town of Whitby, it is one of my favourite places in Yorkshire, and so to be able to go back there in my writing was a joy.

Over the course of the next couple of years, all the while writing and publishing other works, I started to slowly build up a profile of Matthews, and start to plan out a new case for him. At the end of 2017 I finally started work on The Planting of the Penny Hedge, and over the course of a year worked on character building and plot.

My love of writing usually sees me do minimal planning of plot (and maximum historical researching) as I enjoy seeing where a story takes me; however with this book I had to be much more detailed and planned out so I knew exactly where to leave the clues that would eventually see the murderer caught. It has so far been my longest project (both time and word count) and I am thrilled with the final result. I hope you like it too.

About The Author

Chris Turnbull was born in Bradford, West Yorkshire, before moving to Leeds with his family. Growing up with a younger brother, Chris was always surrounded by pets, from dogs, cats, rabbits and birds…the list goes on.

In 2012 Chris married his long term partner, since then Chris has relocated to the outskirts of York where he and his partner bought and renovated their first home together.

Chris now enjoys his full time employment at the University of York and spends his free time writing, walking his Jack Russell, Olly, and travelling as much as possible.

For more information about Chris and any future releases you can visit:

www.chris-turnbullauthor.com
facebook.com/christurnbullauthor
Twitter: @ChrisTurnbull20
Instagram.com/Chris.Turnbull20

Acknowledgements

I would firstly like to thank my long suffering husband, who as always is so supportive of my writing projects.

I would also like the thank Angelina Smith for being the first reader of this book and giving me some great feedback…thank you for also keeping the title and content a secret too.

I would like to thank Joseph Hunt for the fantastic book cover design, it has been great fun working with you on the three 'D' book covers and now this.

I would like to thank Dawn Singh for her continued support, she is the sole reason I became a published author and I cannot thank her enough for encouraging me to go for it.

Lastly I would like to thank all the people who have read and enjoyed my books, it is an honour to read your reviews and see that you are enjoying what I do too.

Thank You!

Eagle of The Empire
Book 1 of the Relic Hunters series

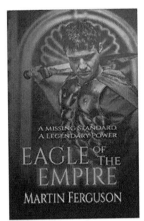

Relic Hunters is a treasure seeking adventure series in which historical tales are interwoven with modern days adventures.

EAGLE OF THE EMPIRE

When his brother mysteriously disappears, sixteen-year-old Adam Hunter will discover that the stories he was told as a boy have more truth to them than he ever thought possible.

To free his brother, Adam must discover the truth about the lost Roman Ninth Legion and find its fabled Eagle Standard, an artefact of mysterious mythical power. Adam will not have to do this alone, calling on the help of the covert teams of the British Museum, specialists who find and protect relics around the world.

Adam Hunter and the British Museum will need to act fast to stop an immortal tyrant who seeks to claim the Eagle of the Empire and with it bring the world to its knees.

www.martinfergusonauthor.com

Printed in Poland
by Amazon Fulfillment
Poland Sp. z o.o., Wrocław